# Sweet Love on the Cove

## A LATER IN LIFE ROMANCE

### CHICKADEE COVE TRILOGY
### BOOK THREE

### ELIZA ESTER

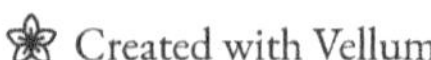 Created with Vellum

# Chapter One

J eannie's hands were freezing. The air in the room had become twice as cold, and despite that, she was burning up inside. She could feel the hairs on her skin rise, forming a rough layer on the goose bumps all over her. It was almost as if someone had pushed a pause button. Everything in the room stood still. Quiet. She could even hear her own heartbeat loud and clear. The feeling was all too familiar...something she had experienced sixteen years ago.

"Where's Lily?" Jeannie asked him with a quivering voice.

"*We are unsure currently, ma'am. However, seeing the level of damage done to the car, we will open a case.*"

"Open a case?" Jeannie breathed. "Open...a case?"

The phone slipped from Jeannie's grip and fell to the floor. A case? Not again. Not after the turmoil she had to endure when Lily went missing the first time. That period had been hell. She still had nightmares, and those moments of raw fear were still very vivid in Jeannie's memory. The tears she shed then could have filled a bucket. She was not as agile as she was over a decade ago, and Jeannie was certain she could not endure another police case.

Seeing how distraught Jeannie was, Aaron picked up the phone from the ground. He put it on speakerphone, set it down on the center table, and took Jeannie's trembling hands into his.

"What do you mean, a case?" he asked. "You're going to open a case already?"

"That is correct, Mr. Horn," the officer answered. "We will need Miss Miller to come down to the station so we can complete the report."

"Hang on, officer," Aaron said. "Just last night, I asked that you open a case, but you refused, claiming that it wasn't protocol. Not that I'm complaining, but why are you now willing to launch an investigation when the 48-hour mark has not elapsed?"

"Well, there's evidence on the scene pointing to the likelihood that this was a hit-and-run or a violent kidnapping," the officer explained. "The car didn't run into anything, but it's bashed in and the driver is missing. There's no way she could have walked out of this wreckage by herself, and seeing as she hasn't contacted any of you, we have every cause to believe that there's a case here. So we're starting one. There's every possibility that she is missing. But to be sure we're covering all bases, we will check with hospitals nearby to see if she found her way into one. We are finishing up here at the scene. Once we're done collecting evidence, we'll return to the station to investigate. I will contact you again if we find anything."

"Aaron," Jeannie said, crying. "Aaron, they are going to open a case. Lily is missing again. Someone has taken her. Someone has hurt her. What am I going to do?"

"Relax, Jeannie," Aaron said, squeezing her hand. "We need a level head to figure this out. I promise, we'll figure this out."

"We'll call you when we find something, Mr. Horn," the officer said.

"Thank you," Aaron said. "Please, we will expect your call, officer."

"Will do."

A million thoughts crowded Jeannie's mind, making it difficult for her to think. Her entire body trembled uncontrollably. Jeannie couldn't process all that was going on. Just a couple of hours ago, Lily had walked out of her home. Now, there was every possibility that Lily was seriously hurt.

Missing. Kidnapped. Wreckage. Blood...

Jeannie squinted hard and shuddered. She didn't want to imagine it, but all Jeannie could see was Lily covered in blood somewhere in the woods. Or Lily tied up somewhere at the mercy of a vile person. The thought was terrifying; however, Jeannie couldn't stop herself from imagining it.

"Jeannie," Aaron whispered. "Look at me."

Jeannie kept her eyes shut. "Oh, Jesus."

"Jeannie," Aaron called her again. "Open your eyes and look at me. Please."

"I have a terrible feeling about this, Aaron," she whispered. "Something is wrong. Something is wrong."

"Jeannie," Aaron called her a third time. "Please open your eyes and stop thinking the worst. I know that there's so much you're imagining right now, and all this just seems so terrifying. I also know that this is difficult to ask you, but please, I need you to calm down. We have to stay positive. Lily will be fine. She has to be. Open your eyes and breathe."

Slowly, Jeannie opened her eyes and sniffed hard. She wiped the tears that had fallen on her cheeks and met Aaron's gaze. He seemed calm, but his eyes said something different. Aaron, too, was worried, confused, and on the verge of tears. But it was one of those scenarios where he had to be strong for her. Jeannie stifled the tears as she tried to maintain her composure. Aaron was right. She needed a level head if she was going to find her daughter.

"There's something wrong, Aaron," Jeannie said.

"I know," Aaron said. "But we have to be optimistic. The police have options, so all is not lost. They are still going to collect clues and check hospitals. We need to have faith."

"No, I can feel it. Lily would have called me," Jeannie explained. "She is many things, but Lily is not strong or brave. She gets terrified at the sight of her own blood. There is no way that she was in a car accident and found her way to a hospital."

Aaron hugged Jeannie tightly and caressed her arm. "Jeannie, come on. There is every possibility that Lily found her way to the hospital. You have every right to be worried, but you need to think of your health, too. Worrying isn't good for you, and neither will it help Lily. Let's cover every possibility first before we panic."

Jeannie shook her head. "It's just—think about it, Aaron. The accident happened on a highway. In the middle of the night. The police just confirmed that Lily was bleeding. She couldn't have gone far on her own. She couldn't have gone anywhere at all. The only way she could have left the car is if someone took her out of it."

"Don't think about it like that."

"How else am I supposed to think about it, then?" Jeannie questioned. "It's the only thing that makes sense. Someone took her, Aaron. Someone has my baby, and it is all my fault. If I hadn't agitated her, she wouldn't have left in that state. Who knows what she's going through at this moment? The mere thought of it terrifies me, Aaron."

"I understand that you're scared, but speaking like this will do nothing to help this situation," he explained. "Once the police are done gathering the evidence they need from the scene, they will call us in and tell us everything that they know. Now, all we can do is wait. I know it doesn't seem right to do so, but it's the only option we have."

"It's not," Jeannie said and struggled to her feet. "We can actually do something. I don't know. I can't just sit here and wait, Aaron. My imagination will get the best of me, and it will drive me insane. I need to find Lily."

Aaron rose to his feet, too. "We searched all night, Jeannie. We couldn't find her, and neither could the police. I'm afraid all we can do is wait. We don't have any information to act on. It's like we're in the dark."

"I can't just sit here and wait, Aaron. I have to do something," Jeannie argued.

Aaron threw his hands in the air. "Well, what do you want to do? Tell me what's on your mind."

Jeannie found it hard to exhale. She balled up a chunk of her hair in her fist and paced. "I think I should keep looking. I don't know...I don't think I looked hard enough."

"That is because you fainted," Aaron told her. "You were too weak to continue. But we did. The rest of us searched for as long as we could. We didn't find anything. No sign of Lily."

The waterworks started all over again. Jeannie interlocked her fingers, pacing and crying at the same time. "We couldn't have looked everywhere. She has to be somewhere. I mean, Chickadee Cove isn't a small place. She's somewhere around. I know it."

Aaron tried to grab Jeannie, but she made it impossible with her pacing. Her vision was blurred with her tears, and her knees were on the verge of buckling, but she kept at it, walking up and down the living room with her fingers in her hair.

"It's my fault," she said. "This has happened before, and I can feel it happening again. I should have stopped her. I should have stood in front of the car. I should have forced my way in. I shouldn't have let her leave."

"Jeannie, Jeannie,"—Aaron finally reached her and held her still—"This isn't helping you or Lily. You said this has happened before. Someone has kidnapped Lily before. Did any of this help? Did panicking help you in any way? How will you find Lily if you can't get it together? You need to be strong for your child. I know it's hard, but you have to try."

Jeannie mellowed. Thinking back to the first time Lily went missing, Jeannie realized that all her panicking had done was drive her to the verge of insanity. She did little to help with the investigation because she found it difficult to think and focus. This time, although the situation seemed familiar, it was different. Lily wasn't a baby anymore; times had changed, and Jeannie had changed, too.

Feeling a bit more relaxed, Jeannie dropped her hands to her side and took in a deep breath. "I'm sorry."

"There is absolutely no need for you to apologize to me, Jeannie," Aaron said to her. "I will go out and continue looking for Lily if it will calm you down. I think going to the scene of the accident and searching for clues personally is a good idea. Who knows what I might find?"

"I'll come with you," Jeannie said. "You're right. It's a good idea."

"No, stay home," Aaron told her. "You need to rest, and I think it's best you stay home in case Lily comes back here."

Jeannie shook her head. "I don't think I can bear the silence, Aaron. I want to come along with you. I might find some clues, too, that will help the police with their investigation."

"Jeannie—"

"I'm better now, Aaron," she told him. "Let's go to the highway and look for Lily. I'm coming with you whether you want me to or not."

Reluctantly, Aaron nodded in response. "Alright. We'll go together. But we will search for about an hour and come back home, alright? This is the only place that Lily knows. I think that if she was out there on her own, she'd come here. So, we won't search for long."

Jeannie nodded. "I agree. I'll grab a jacket and we'll be on our way."

***

The car had been towed by the time they arrived at the scene of the accident. Jeannie stood by the side of the highway staring at the dried patch of blood on the ground, the shattered glass, and the skid marks. She fought the urge to break down in tears. Lily must have been in so much pain. She might have broken a bone or two, bled a lot, been stabbed by something sharp...there were so many horrible things that could have happened to her.

"My poor baby," Jeannie sobbed.

"It must have been a drunk driver," Aaron noted, staring at the spot, too.

"Why do you think so?" Jeannie asked, fixating her gaze on the dried blood.

"There's no intersection. It was the middle of the night. The highway had to have been free. Lily was driving in the right lane. How in the world did the accident happen? The only possibility I'm seeing is that the person who did this...he lost control of the wheels in the opposite lane, sped into oncoming traffic, and rammed into Lily's car."

"Or it was deliberate," Jeannie said and glanced at him. "That, too, is a viable option. This person did this on purpose to stop Lily's car and take her."

"I thought I asked you to stop imagining the worst," Aaron said. "I want to believe that Lily wasn't kidnapped.

This was an accident, and Lily is safe somewhere. I choose not to conclude anything horrible until we're certain."

Jeannie sighed. "I'm trying to be optimistic, but…so much has happened to me, Aaron. It's hard to stay optimistic when you get disappointed a lot. I want to think positively, but I can't. Where's Lily? It makes no sense."

"We'll find her," Aaron said. "For now, let's go down into the woods and see if we find anything."

Jeannie clenched her fingers into a fist as they ventured into the woods, walking side by side. A part of Jeannie was convinced that they would not find anything of use searching amidst the trees. But, as Aaron said, the best she could do was stay optimistic. Hopeful. Lily had battled with so many things in her life, and she had won. She wasn't strong physically, but Lily was strong-willed. Resilient, too. If anyone could survive, she could. Jeannie knew this. She just had to believe it.

"If anyone took Lily from me…" Jeannie said as they walked. "If it turns out that someone took Lily to hurt her, I will never forgive them. I will sacrifice the last drop of my blood to make sure that they pay for doing this."

"The police will find the person who caused the accident and make them pay," Aaron told her. "Let's just find Lily first. Everything else will fall into place."

Jeannie turned to Aaron with tear-filled eyes. "Thank you, Aaron. For being here. For helping me. If I were alone right now, I don't know what I'd do. I'm not very good at handling crisis, you see."

"Oh, I know," Aaron told her. "I've seen the way you handle crises and arguments a couple of times. You're terrible at it. But just know that you're not alone in this, alright? This storm, too, will pass. You believe it, don't you?"

Jeannie nodded. "I hope so."

Aaron took Jeannie's hand into his as they continued the search. Jeannie had no idea what exactly she was looking for, but searching was the best option at that moment. The thought of seeing Lily's lifeless body somewhere in the woods crossed her mind, and she whiffled her head vigorously to ward off the intrusive thoughts.

"Think positive thoughts," she whispered to herself with a quaking voice. "Lily is fine. We'll find her. I know we will."

# Chapter Two

"Any luck?"

An hour had gone by before Cathy and her husband, Derek, arrived to help with the search. Jeannie did not know how far they had walked or whether they were walking in circles or following a straight line. She had called Lily's name probably a hundred times in the space of an hour. Her legs were numb, and her shoulders felt heavier than usual.

"No luck," Jeannie answered Cathy lazily. "There's nothing on that side."

Cathy brought both hands to her hips. "Nothing on my side, too. I was hoping to at least see some footprints, or blood, or something. But there's nothing. I'm starting to think Lily didn't come this way, Jeannie. Perhaps we should go back to the highway and check the other side."

Jeannie shook her head. "Lily couldn't have crossed over to the other side of the road injured. If she stumbled into the woods at all, then it has to be in this one."

"What if she was carried into the woods?" Cathy asked as she scanned the area.

"She wasn't," Jeannie answered. "She couldn't have been. I'm trying hard to stay optimistic. No one carried Lily anywhere. We'll find her. Let's just keep searching for clues."

Cathy nodded. "Good. I'm glad you're thinking this way. I'm hopeful and I pray Lily will return to us safe and sound."

Jeannie nodded and took a step forward. "Well, we have checked this area twice. I think it's safe to say that she didn't come here at all. Where's Aaron and Derek?"

"They are checking the other side," Cathy replied. "Apparently, Derek found a sort of...tunnel. They are checking to see if Lily crawled in there or something."

"Why would she,"—Jeannie swallowed—"I think this is a waste of time. Aaron was right. The best option is to just stay at home and wait. Lily only knows my address in Chickadee Cove, so if there is anywhere she could have gone, it would be my house. She always claims that she doesn't need my help, but whenever she is in trouble, she comes to me. I think we should just go home and wait. At least until we hear from the police."

Jeannie's hand trembled. There was nothing they could do anymore, and searching the woods for any signs of Lily was seeming like a terrible waste of time. Why would Lily be here? Why would she go into the woods instead of calling the police, or an ambulance, or her mother?

"I'm so confused," Jeannie said through clenched teeth, on the verge of tears. "Where's Lily? What is happening? I can't understand anything. I thought searching the woods would distract me from my vivid, horrible imagination, but now all I can think of is one thousand things that could have happened to Lily here in the woods. I am so confused, Cathy. I don't know what I should be doing."

Cathy closed the gap between them and patted Jeannie on the back. "Of course. None of this makes any sense. Your daughter is missing, and possibly injured. It's only right that you're confused and you're panicking. But I think you're right. We should probably wait to hear from the police. Walking around these trees for hours is only going to tire you out. Who knows? Lily might be in a hospital somewhere receiving treatment for minor injuries and you're here, wandering in the woods."

"But what if she's not?" Jeannie asked, massaging her temple. "What if the worst-case scenario turns out to be our reality? What if—"

"I thought we were going to remain optimistic?" Cathy asked, tilting her head to the side. "What happened to the positive spirit you had a minute ago? Where did that Jeannie go?"

"That's what I'm saying, I don't know what to do," Jeannie said and paced. "We should be doing something."

Aaron appeared from nowhere and blocked Jeannie's path. He sighed at seeing the look on her face and held her still by the shoulders.

"We've been over this," he whispered, lowering his head to her eye level. "No pacing. Stop overthinking. We don't know anything yet. I think we should go back home. There's nothing here in the woods. We've been walking for a long time, and I'm pretty sure Lily didn't come this far."

"He's right," Derek chimed in. He walked over to Cathy's side and put his arm around her. "Cathy must have told you I love to hike and hunt a lot with my friends, so I'm a fair enough tracker. I'm almost certain that Lily didn't come here. Plus, I checked the scene of the accident. I can't really be a hundred percent sure, because they have towed away the car from the road, but I'm almost certain that Lily wasn't kidnapped."

Jeannie diverted her attention to Derek. "Why do you think so?"

"Well, from the look of things, the car that caused the

accident skidded and rammed into Lily. I can tell from the skid marks on the other side of the road. So, it might have been a drunk driver, someone that lost control of the car, or a car that lost its brakes. Whatever happened, Lily was in an accident. It wasn't planned or premeditated. I'm sure of it. No one has taken her. With that much damage to Lily's car, the perpetrator must have been badly injured, too."

"We don't think you should worry about Lily being taken...again," Aaron said to Jeannie.

"If she hasn't been taken, then where is she?" Jeannie asked. "That's the only thing that makes sense. Lily can't just disappear into thin air."

"She might still be trying to prove a point, you know," Cathy added. "I mean, it's Lily. I know her, too. You said she stormed off from your house, right?"

Jeannie nodded. "She did."

"What if she staggered out of the wrecked car with minor injuries, get a cab, and continue her journey? That is also a possibility."

Jeannie shook her head. "It's not. Like I told Aaron, Lily is not brave."

Cathy snapped her fingers. "Right. She's terrified at the sight of blood. Even her own."

"Exactly," Jeannie said and let out a frustrated sigh. "If she sustained injuries, she'd come home. Immediately."

"You're sure she hasn't outgrown her fear of blood?" Derek asked. "I mean, Lily has tried to kill herself before, hasn't she? That's how impulsive she is."

"Right, but the first time she tried to was the time we found out the sight of blood terrified her. She cut her wrist and then she started yelling for help. I'm sure. If Lily was conscious after the accident, she would be in my arms by now. That's why I'm paranoid. I know my child."

Aaron blew raspberries. "Well, then this is getting even

more complex. Hours have passed. If she was in a hospital, they would have called Jeannie by now."

Jeannie felt tears sting her eyes. "That's why I think—"

"She hasn't been kidnapped," Aaron said, cutting her off. "That it has happened before doesn't mean it's happening again. Calm down, Jeannie. Right now, I think we should go to the police station."

"I agree," Derek said. "They should have answers for us."

"No, I think we should go to Jeannie's house," Cathy argued. "I mean, think about it. Lily could go back there in search of her mother."

"She was in an accident, honey," Derek pointed out. "I don't think she went home."

"Well, you never know."

While the three of them squabbled about the best course of action, Jeannie felt her phone buzz in her pocket. She stepped aside and pulled it out, hoping to God that it was Lily calling.

"You guys," Jeannie said with a quaking voice as she stared at the caller ID. "I don't—I don't know this number. It could be Lily."

"Well, answer it," Cathy said. "Quickly."

Jeannie slid the button on the screen and slapped the phone to her ear. "Lily? Lily, is that you?"

"It's me. My phone died, so I'm calling you with someone else's."

The sound of the all-too-familiar voice irked Jeannie. She could feel the irritation deep in her bones. "What do you want, Luka?"

"Before you cut the call on me, you'd be glad to know that I found our daughter," Luka answered. "I found her in the wrecked car the night before, and I brought her to Chickadee Cove Memorial Hospital."

"What?" was all Jeannie could say.

"Lily has been in surgery for over three hours, Jeannie."

---

As Jeannie scurried into the hospital, followed by her pack of friends, mixed emotions coursed through her body, but one overshadowed the rest. It wasn't the relief that Lily had been found, it wasn't gratitude that she was getting treated, and it wasn't joy that someone hadn't taken her daughter from her.

It was anger.

"How dare you?" Jeannie barked at Luka as she stormed down the hallway.

Luka rose to his feet quickly and put his arm up to shield himself. "Calm yourself, Jeannie. Our daughter is in surgery."

"You are a vile man, Luka Smith," she roared and shoved Luka into the wall.

Aaron stood in front of Jeannie, blocking her from attacking Luka again. "Jeannie, you need to breathe."

"He *knew*," Jeannie told Aaron. "He took her. He knew where she was hours ago and he let me suffer. How dare you?"

"What happened, Luka?" Cathy asked, crossing her arms. "Tell us exactly what happened."

Luka quietly scanned their faces then let out a loud exhale. "I did not expect this reaction from any of you. Shouldn't you be relieved that I found Lily? Why are you all attacking me?"

"You said she has been in surgery for three hours!" Jeannie rasped. "Three hours. And you're just calling me? When did you get here? When did you find Lily? What time did you find her and take her from the scene?"

"Look—"

"When, Luka?" Jeannie asked sternly.

Luka stuffed his hands in his pocket and looked away. "If I remember correctly, it was a little past one in the morning."

Jeannie, Aaron, Cathy, and Derek scoffed simultaneously.

"1 a.m.?" Jeannie repeated. "You took Lily from the car at one in the morning?"

"We were still searching for her at one in the morning," Aaron said, facing Luka. "A ton of us were out in the woods, in the streets, my employees were searching the highways, the bus stations...everyone was searching at 1 a.m. You're saying you found Lily, brought her to this hospital, and didn't think to inform anyone for about eight hours? It never crossed your mind?"

"I needed to make sure she was alright," Luka said.

"No, don't lie, Luka," Jeannie chimed in. "You thought Lily would wake up so you could feed her with your lies before I arrived. But then she had to have surgery, and you realized you couldn't put it off any longer."

"You're making it sound like I'm a monster."

"You *are* a monster!" Jeannie retorted. She turned around, fighting back both the rage and the tears. Aaron took her into his arms and caressed her back, giving her the warmth she needed to gather herself.

After a long pause, Jeannie broke the hug and turned back to Luka. "How is she? What did the doctor say?"

"I'm not sure of anything yet," Luka said. "They were running some tests, checked for injuries, took an MRI, then suddenly the dang machine started beeping and they rushed her into the emergency room."

"Didn't the doctors say anything else?" Jeannie asked, throwing her hands in the air.

"Not yet," he answered. "I was hoping to get answers after the surgery, but I didn't think it would take this long."

"I bet you didn't," Jeannie retorted. She walked to the other side of the hallway, sat on the bench, and dropped her head in her palm.

Her anger seemed to have subsided as relief washed over her. Lily was safe. That was all that mattered in the end.

Jeannie shut her eyes, thankful that all the horrible things she had imagined had not turned into reality. There were a lot of different directions the situation could have gone. Although a part of Jeannie badly wanted to lash out at Luka for being selfish, even when her daughter's life was at stake, Jeannie didn't want to dwell on him. He craved attention, and the more she gave it to him, the more infuriated she was going to be with herself.

Aaron took his seat by Jeannie's side, and before his back touched the chair, Jeannie sunk into his arms. He responded instinctively, stroking her arms to calm her down.

"Let's wait for the doctor before you draw conclusions, Jeannie," Aaron said to her softly. "Alright?"

Jeannie nodded. "At least she's safe. We can deal with anything else that comes our way."

"Yes, we can. Don't let him get to you. At the very least, he brought Lily to safety. His reasoning or logic doesn't matter to you. The bottom line is that Lily is out of harm's way."

"He was being selfish, even when Lily's life was at stake," Jeannie rasped. "What kind of person thinks only of his own benefit all the time? The police have started building a case, people have been out searching for Lily since last night, too. Emily, Mason, and Sarah are all worried sick, and he didn't think to call until after eight hours. That's not a human thing to do. He's sick."

Aaron continued stroking Jeannie's arm. "Don't let it get to you. Remember, your focus here is Lily. Only her."

Jeannie placed her head on Aaron's shoulder and let out a heavy sigh. "You're right. I'm sorry."

"Don't be."

Time went by slowly. Jeannie could hear the ticking of the clock in her head. Her mind had no rest. Two hours went by, but it felt as though they had been seated all day. Then another hour went by before the doors of the ER finally opened.

Jeannie sprung to her feet instantly and stood in the doctor's path with her hands clasped together.

"Good morning, doctor," she managed to say, peeking into the emergency room. "Where's...how is Lily, please? I'm Jeannie. I'm her mother and legal guardian."

The doctor took off his face mask and eyeglasses. "Well, we ran a series of tests prior to the emergency surgery we just did on Miss Lily. We discovered a couple of things. She suffered a cracked skull because of trauma to the head caused by the accident. She also suffered hairline fracture on her humerus, and some internal injuries in her chest area. She was taken into surgery to stop the bleeding, and we have got the situation under control. Lily is stabilized now and is currently in an induced coma."

Jeannie blinked rapidly. "Induced coma?"

"That's correct." The doctor nodded. "I'm afraid she will be unconscious for a couple of days till her body starts to recuperate properly."

"What—what do I do now?" Jeannie stammered, unable to grasp the situation fully. "I can't see Lily?"

"You can," he answered. "She will be checked into a room and set up. All we can do now is wait for her to wake up."

Jeannie staggered back and hyperventilated. "You said the surgery went well?" she breathed.

"It did," the doctor said. "I assure you."

"Then why is she in an induced coma?"

"Jeannie," Aaron said, spinning her around. "She needs to heal. That's what the doctor is saying. Her body needs to repair itself. To do that, she needs to be asleep. But the surgery was a success. She'll be fine."

"She'll be fine?"

"She will." Aaron nodded. "I'll get Lily into one of the best rooms here in the hospital and make sure that she is well taken care of. Don't worry."

Jeannie couldn't control the tears. She broke down completely, wailing as if the doctor hadn't just delivered some good news. It was the relief, coupled with the fact that Jeannie was scared to bits just a few hours ago. Her emotions were all over the place.

"She'll be fine," Jeannie cried. "Lily's fine."

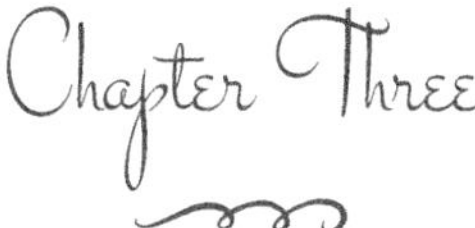

# Chapter Three

"Has she even moved a finger?"

Three days had passed since the incident.

Three days since Jeannie had seen the inside of her own house, her bakery, or even the exit of the hospital. Lily had not moved since she came out of the emergency room, and Jeannie had not moved an inch from her side.

"Wait. Hang on a minute," Jeannie said. She struggled with her camera, trying different angles so her three other children could see Lily's face. "Can you see her well?"

"Mum, just turn the back camera on and point it at Lily," Mason suggested. "It looks like you're trying to take a selfie like this."

"Oh, right. Sorry. Back camera. Why didn't I think of it?"

Jeannie lowered the phone and tapped the screen. Once the camera flipped, she turned it to face Lily on the bed. "Can you see her clearly now?"

Emily clicked her tongue. "She has lost even more weight. At this rate, Lily will become a skeleton if she doesn't wake up soon and eat some solid food," she joked.

"Why does she have dark circles on her eyes?" Sarah asked.

"I mean, she's sleeping. Why would a sleeping person have dark circles?"

"Well, for several reasons," Emily answered. "It could be because of the constricted blood vessels under the eyes, causing hyperpigmentation, or thinning of the skin, also around the eyes. In Lily's case, I'm guessing it's just racoon eyes."

"We get it, professor," Sarah said and sighed dramatically. "I know Lily and I fight sometimes, but—"

"Sometimes?" Mason chipped in. "You both are practically cat and mouse."

"That doesn't matter," Sarah said. "What I'm trying to say is, seeing her like this is just...it hurts. I mean, Lily might be a pain in the backside, but I hate seeing her like this."

"Yeah. Me, too," Emily mumbled. "It's weird seeing her this calm."

"I can't get used to it for the life of me. Lily needs to wake up as soon as possible," Mason said. "What is the doctor saying, mum?"

Jeannie turned the camera to face her. "Nothing," Jeannie answered. "He says I need to be patient. That this is normal, and Lily will wake up at her own time. No one seems to be worried, so I'm trying not to be. From the look of things, Lily seems stable. The doctors haven't found the need to come rushing into the room to treat her, the machines haven't malfunctioned, and the nurses come in twice a day to change her IV bag."

"What about you?" Sarah asked. "You haven't gone home since that day, mum. I mean, if Lily's condition is stable as you claim, then you don't have to be by her side every second of the day. When was the last time you slept on an actual bed?"

Jeannie forced a smile. Everyone had suggested that she go home at one point or another. But Jeannie couldn't bring herself to leave Lily's side. She feared that the moment she stepped out of the hospital, Lily would regain consciousness and be all alone. Given the severity of the accident, Jeannie figured it was best to stay by Lily's side and be there to explain what happened to her when she eventually opened her eyes.

"Oh, you don't need to worry about me at all," Jeannie told them. "I'm perfectly fine. Aaron put Lily in one of the best rooms here at the hospital. This place is practically a mini suite. There's a bathroom here, a nice sofa, cable television. Everything I need is here. What reason do I have to leave?"

"To go home and sleep on an actual bed, mum," Mason said. "You have been sleeping on the sofa for three days straight. That's not healthy. You're going to develop back problems."

"We're not asking you not to be there for Lily," Emily chimed in. "But you can spend the entire day at the hospital and go home at night to rest and freshen up. Then come back in the morning."

"What if Lily wakes up during the night and I'm not here?"

"I'm sure you'll be called," Emily answered.

"You three know how Lily is," Jeannie said, staring at Lily's face. "Remember the last time she was admitted into the hospital and was unconscious for an entire day? When she woke up, she threw a fit. She yanked out the IV from her arm and was too confused to settle down. It took both you and me, Emily, to calm her down and explain to her that her attempt to end her life didn't work. What if she wakes up like that again?"

"I highly doubt the same thing will happen again this time, mum," Emily said. "She has been in a coma for three days. She won't have any energy left in her body to throw a fit. Trust me."

Jeannie dropped her shoulders. "I trust you. But I don't want to risk it, either. I understand you are all worried about my health, and I'm asking you not to be. I'm alright. I promise, if I feel the need to take a break, to go home and rest, I will."

"You promise?" Sarah asked.

"Oh, come on. We know that's a lie," Mason chimed in. "Let's just hope that Lily wakes up soon, for mum's sake. She's not moving an inch from that hospital until she does."

"You're probably right," Sarah concurred. "We'll keep calling to check up on you and Lily, mum. If there is anything you need at all, make sure you call us right away, alright?"

Jeannie nodded. "By the way, Sarah, where are you? I'm sorry, I haven't asked how you three are, or even called to check up on you guys, either. How are you? What have you been up to?"

A brief pause ensued. "Well, we're wrapping up the season," Mason said. "My team is in third place, but that can change, and I'm hoping it will, since our aim is to take home the trophy. Thankfully, I haven't sustained any severe injuries. But my ankles are swollen right now."

"Oh, honey," Jeannie said, holding the phone closer to her face before realizing it wouldn't bring Mason any closer on the screen. "You look tired, too. Are you getting rest at all?"

"How could he be getting rest?" Sarah asked. "He plays in a match practically every day. If he isn't playing, then he's training."

Jeannie stared back and forth at Lily and her phone screen. There was so much going on that she wasn't paying attention to other things in her life. She barely knew what Mason was up to, or where Sarah was, or what Emily was doing. They made it a duty to call her several times a week to inquire about her wellbeing, but Jeannie had been too preoccupied to ask about theirs.

"I'm in Peru at the moment," Sarah revealed. "Hubby has a meeting here this weekend, so I tagged along because I felt like it."

"Peru?" Emily asked. "Do you even still live in New York? At this rate, you'd visit the fifty states before the end of the year."

"When will you be going back to New York to settle down, Sarah?" Jeannie asked her. "You are my only current hope for a grandchild now, you know? Emily and Mason are both married to their professions, and Lily, well...Lily's young."

"Don't worry about that, mum," Sarah said. "I'll give you your grandbaby."

Jeannie chuckled. "Thank you, my darling. Emily? Anything you'd like to tell me? How's work?"

"Work's fine, I guess. There's not a lot going on for me at the moment," Emily answered.

Jeannie nodded. "I'm sorry I don't call to check up on the three of you like I used to. Hopefully, things will go back to normal soon, and all of that will change."

"Oh, come on, mum. It's not like we're toddlers," Sarah replied. "Just take care of your health. Emily, Mason, and I sent you some money. Use it to take care of yourself. We'll send you some more by the end of the week."

"Thank you so much. I love you all very much."

"We love you, too," Emily answered. "Bye, mum."

"Bye," she said and blew kisses.

Once the call ended, Jeannie rose to her feet to check on Lily. Three days was a long time for her to be asleep. But everyone else didn't see anything to worry about, hence she had to remain calm, too. Lily was fine. The doctor had said so himself.

---

"Jeannie? Jeannie, wake up."

Her eyelids were heavier than usual. Jeannie tried to open

her eyes, but the best she could do was bat her eyelids repeatedly. She caught glimpses of a figure squatted by her side by the sofa, and from the rich scent of the perfume the person had on, Jeannie was certain that it was Aaron.

"Aaron," she said lazily. "You're back."

"I am," Aaron said, drawing lines on Jeannie's forearm with his finger. "Are you alright? Have you had anything to eat?"

Jeannie dragged herself up from the sofa and sat. "I'm fine. I had lunch earlier, but I'm not hungry yet, so dinner can wait. Did you just arrive, or have you been here for a while?"

"I just got here," Aaron answered. "You look tired."

Jeannie yawned. "I didn't get much sleep last night," she answered. "I don't know why. I just couldn't stay asleep."

Aaron sat by Jeannie's side and rubbed her back. "Do you want me to get you some medicine to help you sleep? Or perhaps some milk?"

Jeannie shook her head. "No pills, thank you. I'm trying to stay away from taking pills unless they are necessary. It's not that serious. I'll just turn off all the lights this time and take some milk, like you said."

Aaron glanced at the sofa. "I think we should get a bed in here," he suggested. "A small but comfy one that we can easily move around. That way, you don't have to keep sleeping on the sofa. It's our best option since you refuse to go home."

"Aaron, you've already done enough," Jeannie said. "I don't have a problem sleeping on the sofa. I promise, if it gets too uncomfortable, I'll tell you. But I'm fine."

"You just said you find it difficult to sleep."

"That has nothing to do with the sofa," Jeannie argued. "Don't worry about it."

Aaron stared at her in an obvious state of indecision between remaining quiet and saying something else. He sighed and reluctantly threw in the towel. "Fine. I brought you dinner. It's Mexican."

A smile formed on Jeannie's lips. "Oh, thank you. I like Mexican food."

"I know. Now eat something."

"Later," Jeannie groaned. She took the bag from him and placed it on the small table. "Now, tell me about you? How was your day? How was work? What did you do?"

Aaron placed his head on the sofa. "You've asked me that three days in a row. Why don't you tell me about your day this time?"

"There's nothing to tell," Jeannie said. "You know this. My day was uneventful. Tell me about yours. I want to hear about it."

Jeannie leaned her head on the sofa, too, and stared directly into Aaron's eyes with a smile on her face. They were ignoring the obvious elephant in the room. Lily's incident had brought them back together, and it appeared they had made up even without talking about their relationship. Jeannie blamed it on poor timing. Aaron wouldn't want to bring it up because there were more pressing matters at hand. Jeannie sensed Aaron was waiting for her to talk about it. She, on the other hand, liked how things were between them. She was scared that bringing up their argument, and the reasons they separated in the first place, was going to create a gap between them all over again. A gap that Lily's accident had closed.

Amidst all the confusion caused by the accident, Jeannie was sure of one thing. Her feelings for Aaron were strong. Certain. The last three days had really shown her that Aaron was the man of her dreams. Their quiet conversations in Lily's hospital room lasted for hours, and Jeannie fell asleep better in Aaron's arms. He knew the right words to say to encourage and soothe her, and he was always there, even though he was a busy man.

"How about we make a deal then?" Aaron asked, adjusting in his position.

Jeannie's eyebrows furrowed. "What deal?"

"I will tell you all about my day, the new clients we have, and how work is going if you have breakfast with me at a nice diner tomorrow."

"Are you asking me out, Aaron Horn?" she questioned teasingly.

"Would you feel better if it wasn't a date?" he asked. "I just want you to get some fresh air, Jeannie. It's only breakfast. I'll have you back here at the hospital in two or three hours."

Jeannie glanced at Lily and then turned her attention back to Aaron. The least she could do was put in an effort before she ruined things with him again. Besides, she really needed some fresh air. A walk would do her some good, too, given that she had barely left the hospital room for anything.

"I'd love to, Aaron," Jeannie answered with a smile.

## Chapter Four

"It's been a week, Aaron. I think it's only reasonable that I worry."

The aromatic scent of flowers filled Jeannie's nose as they strolled by a floral shop in the center of town. It was the third time in four days that they had gone to Wendy's for breakfast. Jeannie didn't think she'd be out of Lily's room that often, but she found it hard to turn Aaron down anytime he asked her out for breakfast. It was his attempt to distract her from Lily's state, and Jeannie was thankful for it. Most of the time, it worked. They would spend the morning talking about everything else, about Aaron's work, what he was up to...

The bakery was also running smoothly thanks to him and Cathy. They had squeezed out time to run it in her stead. Her employees also made it easy for Jeannie to be at the hospital. They would sometimes video call Jeannie and show her how busy the store was or ask questions about her recipes. Everyone was doing so much to make Jeannie's life easier. Just thinking about it brought her to the edge of tears. There was so much she was grateful for. Sometimes she wondered if she had been a hero in her past life to have earned so many good people around her now who made her wellbeing their priority.

Aaron placed both hands on Jeannie's shoulders and guided her away from the road. "The doctor says Lily is stable for now, but they cannot tell us anything until she wakes up."

"That's exactly my point," Jeannie said. She took a sip from the already melted iced latté in her hand and sighed softly. "Why does it feel like I'm exaggerating when this should be a cause for concern? It's been seven days. She's been in a coma for seven days, and the doctors don't think it's a big deal."

"They are doctors, Jeannie. I'm sure they have handled this sort of situation before. I mean, it's what they studied in school, is it not? If they say there is no cause for concern, then I don't see why you should start panicking."

"I read about something like this on Google," Jeannie revealed. "If Lily is in a coma for too long, then she might become a vegetable. That's brain death, Aaron, and she has been like this for a week. I mean, how long is too long?"

"Have the doctors mentioned anything about Lily falling into a vegetative state?" Aaron asked.

"Well, no, but—"

"But nothing," Aaron said to her. "Goodness, Jeannie. You worry way too much over things you cannot control. There is nothing we can do right now but wait for Lily to wake up on her own, but you are worrying like the doctors have announced that Lily is dying."

"I have nothing to do but worry, Aaron," Jeannie said. "What else am I going to do with all the time on my hands? I overthink, I can admit that, but you have to admit that I have every right to be worried."

"You do, but this isn't just worry," Aaron said. "What you are is paranoid. You have a vivid imagination, Jeannie, and you use it to think up horrible things. You're not a very optimistic person."

"Well, can you blame me? My life hasn't been that rosy or filled with opportunities. Every single time I have been optimistic in the past, my hopes have been shattered. What I do is, I think of the worst that can happen, so when something good happens instead, I am pleasantly surprised."

Aaron paused abruptly and arched his eyebrows. "That is just weird, Jeannie Miller."

Jeannie giggled and stood in front of him. "Why? I like surprises. Pleasant surprises."

"Well, no...I don't think you should,"—Aaron swallowed —"You have a weird logic, Jeannie. I am so confused. Why would you think the worst so you can be pleasantly surprised when something good happens? You can still be pleasantly surprised if you hope for the best."

Jeannie tilted her head to the side. "You're telling me you don't do the same thing?"

Aaron shook his head. "Not at all. I like to be hopeful. Very hopeful."

"Well, what do you do when things don't happen the way you wanted them to? I mean, if you're too hopeful, you won't see it coming."

"If things don't work out how I want them to, I get disappointed. That's normal. I don't enjoy thinking of the worst that could happen."

"Well, I don't like to, either, but I can't help that I think about it first before anything else," Jeannie said and shrugged her shoulders. "How do I explain it...it's like covering the ground, making sure you have thought about every single possibility before the result comes in. For me, when I'm hopeful and things don't work out how I planned it to, I get heartbroken. Sometimes I cry, and it hurts. I don't like to be caught off guard, that's all."

Aaron crossed his arms. "I'm pretty sure there is a psychological term for this. I just don't know what it is."

"Don't get me wrong, Aaron. I hate it when things don't go as planned," Jeannie explained. "It's not the same with Lily. For Lily, I pray every single day that she wakes up and talks to me. But I also need to know every single thing that might go wrong, so I can pray about it and be prepared to tackle it."

"Luka did this to you," Aaron said, catching her off guard. "The constant disappointment did this to you, I'm sure of it. It has forced you to guard your heart, so it doesn't suffer another heartbreak again."

"Alright, now you're jumping the gun," Jeannie said and continued walking.

"I think I'm right. Remember what you told me when I started to like you?" Aaron asked. "You said you didn't come to Chickadee Cove in search of a relationship. You came to start a bakery."

"Okay...so?"

"You had totally given up on the idea of love, Jeannie. I think that's because the same person has hurt too you many times. You know, once bitten, twice shy...but in your case—"

"Don't say it." Jeannie chuckled. "I know I was bitten repeatedly. You don't have to remind me. I live with the shame every day. You might be right, but you could be wrong, too. However, you should know that I am working on myself, and I hope I become that optimistic person that I strive to be."

"I have a feeling you will be soon," Aaron said to her. "Once Lily wakes up, you'll see that you had no reason to be worried at all."

Jeannie sighed. "I hope so, Aaron."

Aaron met her gaze, and she looked away quickly to hide the blush that had formed on her cheeks. Breakfast with Aaron was now the only activity she looked forward to doing every day. She loved their walks. It was the perfect opportunity for her to clear her head and have a laugh.

"The weather is nice out today," Aaron noted.

Jeannie glanced at the sky. She smiled in response and stared at Aaron's hand. Jeannie fiddled with her fingers as she contemplated reaching for him and holding his hand. Was it too forward? Too soon? She didn't want to catch him off guard.

Before she could decide, Aaron's phone rang in his pocket. He reached for it quickly, and when his voice changed after accepting the call, Jeannie knew he had to go.

"Jeannie, I am so—"

"Don't apologize, Aaron," Jeannie said to him. "You are a busy man, and I am grateful that you sacrifice your time to be with me. Go. Don't worry about me."

"I apologize," he said. "I'll be as quick as I can, and I'll make sure to come back soon."

"Aaron, don't inconvenience yourself because of me. I want you to come back, but if you can't, then it's fine."

"I want to," Aaron said. "I'll see you tonight."

Jeannie instinctively smiled. "See you tonight, Aaron."

Aaron took a step forward and jerked back. He spread his arms, then clenched his hands into a fist and dropped them awkwardly. Jeannie was certain he was going in for a hug, but then he changed his mind.

"See you," he said and patted her shoulders.

"Wait, your car is parked at the hospital," she said. "Where are you going? We can just walk there together."

"I'll just take a cab, then come back for it when I return to see you," Aaron said. "Bye, Jeannie."

"Bye," she said inaudibly.

The elephant in the room was getting bigger and bigger by the day. Jeannie watched Aaron hail a cab and hop in. He was unsure of where they stood and probably confused, too. They hadn't addressed their differences, and suddenly, they were talking like nothing had happened. It was weird.

She had to clear the air, or else the gap would form again on its own.

<hr>

The day passed by even slower than usual. However, the minute Jeannie closed her eyes for a quick nap, she woke up at nighttime. But even after so many hours of sleep, Jeannie still felt drained. She jumped into the shower for a quick bath and a change of outfit before Aaron arrived. It had been four days since she last washed her hair, and she wanted to look pretty for Aaron that evening. They were going to talk about their relationship. She wanted to look her best...or at least, the best she could.

Jeannie stared at the sofa as she towel-dried her hair. Sleeping on it had left a dent right in the middle. Just like Mason had predicted, Jeannie was already feeling back pains from constantly sleeping in a fetal position. She didn't want to complain to anyone or take any medication for it, either.

Jeannie turned to stare at Lily. "Lily, darling. Please wake up. Mum's back hurts from sleeping on the sofa. For someone who hated being idle, you sure have been asleep for a long time."

Jeannie crashed on the sofa and picked up her phone. Denise made it a point of duty to send videos of the shop every single day to show Jeannie how things were going. She'd show customers making orders, the crowd seated at the bakery, the workers...everything. It was their little way of assuring Jeannie that they had everything under control. Jeannie had Aaron to thank for his keen eye. During the interview, he had advised Jeannie on her choices. In fact, Jeannie hired all the people he had selected. It turned out that he had been right about them. They were amazing people. Jeannie couldn't have asked for better workers.

A knock on the door distracted her from the video. Jeannie paused and turned just in time to see Aaron walk in. "Aaron," she said with a sigh of relief. "You made it."

"I told you I would," he said and sat by her side. "I brought pizza and wine."

Jeannie watched him set the box down on the table and open it. She shook her head, amused by the excitement in Aaron's eyes. "I don't get why you like pizza so much."

"I don't get how you don't," he said and leaned back. "Thinking about it, what do we have in common?"

His question surprised Jeannie. She wasn't sure what he meant. Was he rethinking the attraction? Had she said something that was slowly driving him away?

"I like pizza," Jeannie stuttered. "I'm just not obsessed with it, like you are."

"I'm not obsessed. It's just the easiest...most delicious thing to eat," he answered.

"I like wine," Jeannie said. She lifted her legs and hugged them to her chest. "You like wine, too, right?"

"I definitely do," he said. "I like the beach."

"I'm obsessed with the beach," Jeannie said, giggling. "See? We do have things in common."

"Yes, we do..." Aaron said.

A long silence ensued between them. Jeannie nibbled her lower lip and looked everywhere except at Aaron's face. The silence was her cue to bring up the discussion that they had been putting off. But Jeannie couldn't bring herself to say anything.

"I know what you're thinking," Aaron finally said, breaking the long pause. "We haven't had time to talk about us and where we stand. I understand why, and we don't have to rush it, Jeannie. I'd like to think that we have somewhat of an understanding now, so let's just…take things slow until we can talk about it. About us."

"We need to address it, Aaron," Jeannie said softly. "You are hesitating because you're not sure we are what we used to be. And it's my fault."

"I never said that. All I'm saying is I understand we cannot talk about it right now."

"I want to talk about it now," Jeannie said to him. "There's no need putting it off when it's creating this gap between us already."

Aaron inhaled deeply and turned to face Jeannie. "Alright, I'm listening. Where do we stand, Jeannie?"

A lump instantly formed in Jeannie's throat. "Let me start by apologizing to you, Aaron. I'm deeply sorry for hurting your feelings."

"You don't have to apologize. That is long forgotten."

"No, it isn't. And you know it," Jeannie said. "You are still offended. It's alright to admit that I offended you. I know I did, and I'm certain that if I were in your shoes, I wouldn't forgive me so easily, either."

"Well, it's easy for me. It's just how it is," Aaron said. "I am not upset, Jeannie. I was offended, but…actually, I'm still offended. But because I understand, it's hard to stay upset."

"Can I be honest with you, Aaron?" Jeannie asked. "Don't answer, sorry. That was a rhetorical question. I honestly think I don't deserve you. I know telling you this might make you reflect on why you're with me in the first place, but…it's the truth. I don't know what I did, or what you like about me. I mean, look at you, then look at me. On top of all this…on top of all you do for me, all I do in return is hurt you or disappoint you. It's embarrassing. I'm ashamed to say that at forty-seven years old, I'm new at this. I've only known one man my entire life. The definition of love that I was exposed to years ago is way different from the definition you're currently teaching me. I take advantage of it because I think it'll go away. No matter how much I think about it, I don't know how to match your energy when it comes to love. It's like you're always going to be at the losing end while I get everything from you."

Aaron watched her speak keenly and then lowered his head when she was done talking.

"That's what you don't understand, Jeannie. I'm not losing. I don't see you every day because it's a chore. I do it because you make me happy. If I'm happy, then what else matters? You make me happy, and I'm not asking you for anything else. I enjoy being around you. I told you from the very beginning. It might not make sense to you, but it does to me. You are not responsible for my happiness. I am. I do all of this because seeing you smile makes my heart race."

Jeannie literarily felt her heart soften up inside. She clenched her teeth as tears filled her eyes.

"I'll do better, Aaron," Jeannie said. "I'm sorry for disappointing and embarrassing you. It was truly not my intention to make you feel awful when all you ever did was try to help me. Please accept my apology."

Aaron took her hand in his. "Apology accepted. I admit your actions hurt me, and I was jealous because I wanted you to choose me over him."

"Aaron—"

"I know," Aaron said. "I know you weren't thinking of it that way. You weren't choosing him over me. You were just trying to help a person in need. My feelings for you have not changed, and they don't intend to. However, if I'm to be completely honest with you. What happened cannot repeat itself. I don't want to get hurt like that ever again. It felt terrible."

"It won't," Jeannie assured him.

"You need to sort out your feelings first so we know where

we stand," Aaron explained. "I know you don't love Luka anymore, but you admit he affects you. That alone is enough to be a problem. I'll do anything for you, Jeannie, but sorting out your feelings is one thing I cannot do."

Jeannie scooted over to Aaron's side and tightened her grip on his hand. "Whatever ties I had with Luka are severed and that bridge is burnt. I hate him at the moment, but what I have learnt in the past few days is that I don't want to hate Luka. I want to be indifferent, and I'm on the right path. I'll do better, I promise. Just trust me this once."

"I trust you," Aaron said, almost in a whisper.

Jeannie dropped her gaze as she traced lines on the back of Aaron's hand. "And Isabel?"

"Isabel?"

"I see you rekindled your relationship with her after we… after our argument," Jeannie explained. "What was that about?"

"Ah." Aaron chuckled. "Isabel. That was nothing, I assure you. Isabel called me one night and said she wanted to call a truce. She wanted to be friends again."

Jeannie's eyebrows furrowed. "Friends? Who stays friends with their ex?"

"Lots of people," Aaron said and shrugged his shoulders.

"What? So you said yes?"

"I did."

Jeannie felt the heat rise in her neck. "You did? So, you're friends with Isabel now?"

Aaron nodded. "Good friends."

"Oh." Jeannie adjusted uncomfortably in her seat. "Well, we all need friends."

"Jeannie, is that jealousy I sense?" Aaron asked, smirking. "If your eyes had lasers, I bet they'd fry me right now."

"Jealous? Who? Me? I'm not. It's just, weird, that's all," Jeannie stammered. She was beyond jealous.

As she turned to look away, Aaron pinched her jaw softly and turned her to face him. He pressed a kiss to her lips and stroked her cheek with his fingers.

"I was kidding," Aaron said as soon as he broke the kiss. "Isabel just said she wanted to be friends to be close to me. I knew her intentions toward me, but I still played along to make you jealous."

"Really?" Jeannie asked, hiding a smirk.

"Really. I wanted you to miss me."

"Well, it worked," she answered. "I was jealous. Especially in church. But now that we have established where we stand, I want you to know that I love you, Aaron, and I don't want to see Isabel anywhere near you again."

Aaron smiled. "I'm sorry, what did you say? I didn't quite hear you."

Jeannie rolled her eyes. "I said...I love you, Aaron."

Aaron pulled Jeannie by the waist and hugged her tightly.

"I love you, too, Jeannie."

# Chapter Five

Ten days.

Jeannie bit her fingers as she paced up and down Lily's hospital room. She was slowly losing it. The worrying was eating her up inside. No one else was sensing the urgency like she was. Lily had not moved on her own in ten days. The nurses were the ones who came in every single day to turn Lily to the side and move her around.

Seeing Lily move only with the help of someone else scared Jeannie. She didn't look alive. Jeannie had thought that Lily would be out of the coma three days after the surgery, but it had been almost two weeks. Two entire weeks of waiting for Lily to open her eyes.

"Good morning, Miss Miller."

Jeannie stopped in her tracks and turned to face the doctor. "Good morning, Dr. Mendel. I've been expecting you."

Dr. Mendel adjusted his eyeglasses and smiled. "I heard," he answered and went straight to Lily to do a routine check.

Jeannie waited patiently while he checked Lily, keeping her

distance so he had his space. Once he was done, he placed his stethoscope back around his neck and faced her.

"Everything looks pretty normal," he said to her.

"No, I don't think it's normal, Dr. Mendel," Jeannie answered. "That's exactly what you've been saying for the last ten days. I know you're doing your best, and I know I shouldn't be questioning your expertise, but hasn't Lily been in a coma for too long? Isn't there a way to wake her up or something?"

"Miss Miller, all I can ask you to do is wait," he said. "Some people stay in a coma for months."

"What? So, you're saying Lily might be like this for months?"

"I'm not saying that," he clarified. "All I'm saying is, Lily's body hasn't fully repaired itself. She's still recuperating. Healing. It might not seem like it, but she is. It's just slower than you expect it to be. Let's wait a little longer and trust me. I'm the doctor here, and I derive no joy in lying to you, or hurting Lily. I want her to be alright, too."

Jeannie mellowed. She threw her hands in the air, then slapped her palm to her forehead. "I'm sorry that I'm like this, Dr. Mendel. I'm not questioning you, I'm just concerned, and I always feel this need to be doing something. These days, I find it difficult to wait or be idle."

"Then go home, Miss Miller. Go to work," Dr. Mendel suggested. "Staying here like this isn't good for you at all. You're cooped up in this hospital, barely getting any direct sunlight. When was the last time you set foot in your house?"

"I can't leave Lily's side, Doctor," she breathed. "I'll go home once she's awake."

"You won't take my advice, huh?" he asked, stuffing his hands in his lab coat.

"I'm sorry," Jeannie whispered, smiling. "But I will take

extra care of my health. Don't worry. I have to stay strong for Lily."

Dr. Mendel nodded. "Alright then," he said and nodded. "If you need anything, you know where to find me. I'll be back to check up on Lily later in the day. I'm going to be running some routine tests on her just to be extra sure we covered everything."

"Alright then," Jeannie said. "Thank you, Dr. Mendel. I sincerely appreciate your help."

Jeannie sat on the side of the bed and took Lily's hand into hers. She stared at her daughter's still face. Her lips were a bit chapped, her skin was pale, as usual, and the purple circles under her eyes were becoming more and more visible.

"Come on, Lily. Wake up," Jeannie said. "Are you doing this to punish me? Because it's working. You're a strong girl, heal quickly and wake up. You know you have that acting job back in New York, and the modelling...there's so much you wanted to do, remember? I'll let you do it all. I won't interfere anymore or complain. So just wake up, alright?"

Jeannie dropped her shoulders. She wasn't sure Lily could even hear her, but she made it a point of duty to talk to her every day. She hoped that somehow, Lily heard her voice and sensed her worry.

"The person who did this to you is still out there, you know?" Jeannie continued. "The police haven't found him yet. The car had no license plates, so it's difficult to trace it. But they are trying. I'm hopeful that soon they'll find this guy and bring him to justice. You should be awake long before then to see it happen. Or even tell us what happened and what you saw. A lot of people are worried about you, Lily. We're rooting for you."

Jeannie returned to the sofa and laid down with her gaze still fixed on Lily. She didn't know what else to do. It was all up to Lily now. All she could do was stay by her side and be there whenever she woke up from her deep slumber.

---

Instead of Aaron's usual nightly visits, Jeannie was graced with Cathy's presence. Aaron was too occupied with work. He had called earlier in the day to tell Jeannie he couldn't make it to the hospital. He promised to make up for it the next day, so Jeannie agreed. She could understand that he was busy with his meetings, but she wanted to see him. Given how much time they had spent together in the last couple of days, Jeannie had grown even more attached to Aaron. So much that she always wanted to be around him.

"I stopped by the bakery 0n my way here," Cathy said, taking a bite from her muffin. "I brought you some cupcakes and a sausage roll. You're welcome."

Jeannie gave Cathy a knowing look. "Did you pay for these, Cathy?"

Cathy scoffed and stuffed her mouth with food. "Why would I pay for these? I'm friends with the owner. I can have as many muffins as I want."

"I see you want the owner to go bankrupt," Jeannie said. "You couldn't even support my business by paying for two muffins, one cupcake, and one sausage? Huh, Cathy?"

Cathy paused. "Fine. I'll pay next time," she said. "Now, eat."

"I was kidding," Jeannie said. "Please, take all the muffins you want, my dear friend. You have done so much for me that a truckload of muffins won't even make up for it."

Cathy blushed and attempted to cover her face with the muffin. "Thank you. But I will pay when I can. I love your muffins, Jeannie. I can eat them every day."

"Thank you," Jeannie said. "How's Travis? How's his health? Is he getting any better?"

Cathy nodded and set the half-eaten muffin down. "I honestly don't know what goes through Travis's mind. Ever since we got back home from the hospital, he has been all over the place. The doctor said he needs to take things slow until we figure out a course of action, but Travis refuses to stay in one place. I feel too bad for him, so it's hard to say no to him, and then again, he needs to stop playing all the time. I honestly have no idea what to do with him. We have to go back to the hospital soon for more tests. But for now, we're doing fine, I guess."

"Thank God," Jeannie said. "You're a strong woman, Cathy. I'm proud of you. You're handling this so well. Better than me, even. I mean, your son has a rare heart condition, and you manage to do it all. You take care of your two other daughters, your husband, you even help me with the bakery, you take time to check on me, bring me a change of clothes, food...you stay by my side and try to console me. I don't know how you do it, but I really want to be like you. I want to be strong like you. All I do is worry and imagine all the worst things in the world that could happen to me."

Cathy must have sensed the serious tone in Jeannie's voice. She moved closer on the sofa and interlocked her fingers together. "Jeannie, the fact that I don't show how terrified, worried, and confused I am doesn't mean that I'm not. You wear your emotions on your sleeve. That's not a bad thing, and it doesn't make you weak. You are valid to react the way you are. Come on. Considering the hand life dealt you, I completely understand how your mind works. Why you worry a lot and lower your expectations. All of that is going to change. Isn't that part of the reason you moved here to Chickadee Cove in the first place? To become a better person and chase your dreams? You will do all of that. All these things that are happening are just steppingstones. Lily will soon regain consciousness, and you'll go back to the shop and run it like you should. Everything will be fine. For the both of us."

"I made so many mistakes, Cathy," Jeannie said. "So many. Everything that is happening right now results from many poor decisions I made. Many naive, stupid decisions. I was trying to be a 'good person.' What a joke. Who was I fooling? If I had just told Luka off at the very beginning. If I had shut it down with him immediately when he came, then he would never have summoned the courage to bring Lily here. If I had told Lily from the start, sternly, that her father and I were never getting back together. If I had told her from the start that Luka caused everything that happened to her...Cathy, Lily's issues started after that incident."

"I know." Cathy nodded. "I know more than anyone else."

"She was a happy child," Jeannie said with a quivering voice. "She was happy, Cathy. She was so full of life. So jolly. Then Luka abandoned her to go drinking and only God knows who took her that day, what they did to her, and why they abandoned Lily in a trash bin. Since that incident, Lily became different. Impulsive. She stopped smiling. She was traumatized. So traumatized that she forgot everything, almost as if her brain hit the reset button. Till this day I still cannot understand how a thirteen-year-old child can be diagnosed with depression. At thirteen!"

"Jeannie, don't start crying now," Cathy said, patting her on the arm.

"I told myself I'd never forgive Luka for what he did to Lily," Jeannie continued. "Still, I let him fool me yet again. And this happened. Lily is lying there because I didn't keep my word."

"You live, you learn," Cathy voiced. "Keep your head up, Jeannie. We will overcome this, like we do everything else. You'll see. Lily is going to wake up, and she'll only get better.

Now that you have seen the kind of person Luka is, you know not to trust him anymore. If he can lie about something as serious as cancer just to get to you, then he isn't someone we should let into your life for any reason at all. It's all for the sake of your mental health. Focus on yourself, Jeannie. You can't take care of everyone else until you care for yourself."

"When Lily wakes up, everything is going to change," Jeannie said. "We are going to have to sit down and talk about her and her future. I think I should tighten my grip on Lily instead of letting her do whatever she wants. That's the only way I can help her."

"I agree," Cathy said. "Let's focus on the positive, alright? I know it might not seem like there's a lot to be thankful for, but if we sit down to count them one by one, you'll see that there's tons of reasons for you to be grateful."

"Thank you, Cathy," Jeannie whispered.

# Chapter Six

"So, when is your trip going to be?"

"In two days," Aaron answered. "I should be gone for about three or four days. Are you going to miss me?"

Jeannie unwrapped the to-go packs Aaron had brought with him for lunch. This time, they were having black bean noodles and some side dishes that Jeannie hadn't opened up yet. She started by placing the drinks on the table, then she took out the two packs of noodles and handed one over to Aaron.

"Of course, I'll miss you," Jeannie answered, fiddling with her chopsticks. "Your plan worked."

Aaron tilted his head to the side. "My plan. What plan?"

"To make me attached to you," Jeannie said. "That was your plan, wasn't it? Now I get sad when you're not around. Who knows how I'll survive the four days you'll be gone, since I'm so used to seeing you every day?"

Aaron scoffed. "Are you messing with me? Or are you being serious?"

"What? I'm being serious."

"You're really going to miss me?"

"I'm really going to miss you," Jeannie assured him. "I'm not going to deny or hide it. I've gotten used to seeing you every single day."

"Well, that's pleasing to know. No worries, I'll make sure I call you every day, because I'll miss you, too. If I had my way, I wouldn't go at all. But I have to be there to close the deal in person, so I'm going."

"To where this time?" Jeannie asked, slurping her noodles.

"Miami," he answered. "It's a quick trip to Miami. I'm meeting with some potential investors and clients."

"Oh, Miami," Jeannie said and nodded. "Are you just going for business, or do you plan on taking a trip to the beach to unwind?"

Aaron scoffed and shook his head. "No, thank you. There will be no unwinding for me. I'm just going for the meeting and coming back to Chickadee Cove for another meeting."

"You work too much, Aaron. When do you take out time for yourself to de-stress and recharge your energy?"

"I'm doing that right now," he replied. "I'm de-stressing right now."

"Really?"

"Really." He smiled. "How's your back, Jeannie? Does it still hurt?"

Jeannie arched her back and stretched. "A bit, but it's more of an ache. I took some"–Jeannie paused and her eyebrows furrowed, realizing that she had not told Aaron about her backache–"How did you find out?"

"Isn't it inevitable?" he asked. "Your back was bound to start hurting at some point. You've been sleeping on a sofa for two weeks now. You won't listen to me when I ask you to go home and rest."

"It's nothing, Aaron. Trust me," Jeannie said. "Besides, it's already too late to leave. I think Lily might wake up soon."

"Jeannie—"

"Must we argue about this every single time we are together, Aaron?" Jeannie asked. "I know you're only looking out for me, but I'm telling you, I'm perfectly fine."

"You don't listen."

Jeannie started to reply when she felt something trickling down her nose. She instinctively pushed her head back and blocked it with a finger.

"Is your nose...bleeding?" Aaron asked, pulling her hand away so he could see. "Jeannie, your nose is bleeding."

"I see that. Can I please get a tissue?" Jeannie asked.

Aaron scrambled around the room searching for a tissue. There was none in the room itself, so he scurried into the bathroom and emerged shortly after with a rolled-up piece of tissue paper.

"Let me see," he said. Without giving Jeannie room to react, Aaron took her hand away from her face and mopped the blood himself.

"I can do it," Jeannie tried to protest.

"Stay still," he demanded. "I can't believe this."

From his furrowed forehead, his fixated, piercing eyes, and the click of his tongue, Jeannie could tell that Aaron was mad. To her, it was just a nosebleed. Everyone had them from time to time. But Aaron saw something else. He was probably thinking that somehow, sleeping on the sofa had something to do with it. Jeannie had given him something else to worry about.

"Aaron," Jeannie said and cleared her throat.

"Don't, Jeannie," he said, focused on blocking the flow of blood from both her nostrils.

"It's just a nosebleed. Everyone has them."

"When was the last time you had a nosebleed?"

"I don't recall."

"Exactly."

"I'm fine."

"I never want to hear you say that to me, Jeannie, when it's obvious that you are not. Stop."

Jeannie took the tissue from him and dropped her head. "Alright," she mumbled. "I admit I am under a lot of stress. I mean, it's obvious why. That is probably the cause of this. Stress."

Aaron took his seat by her side. "The last time I had a nosebleed, I was diagnosed with HBP. I've been on medication since then. You used to complain of headaches, too."

"That was before," Jeannie said. "Now, I don't have them as much as I used to."

Aaron raised his eyebrows. "As much? So, you still have them?"

"They come and go," Jeannie answered. "But don't we all have headaches from time to time? And nosebleeds? It'll pass. Once Lily wakes up, I'll make sure I take a nap for two days straight."

"That's if you don't collapse before Lily opens her eyes," Aaron said. "I need you to run some tests, Jeannie."

Jeannie scoffed and dropped the tissue. "What are you, a doctor?"

"I'm being completely serious, Jeannie," Aaron told her with a straight face. "We need to run some tests to make sure you're fine like you constantly claim you are. There's no harm here. We are already in the hospital, and it won't take long at all."

"Aaron, it's nothing. Let's just eat, alright? We've been over this."

"Would you please listen to me for once, Jeannie?" Aaron asked, visibly annoyed. "Just this once. I'm not asking you to leave the hospital or leave Lily's side. Your nose is bleeding, you're having backaches and constant headaches. Would it kill you to just spare an hour to run some tests and make sure you're in good shape?"

Jeannie mellowed, sensing the concern and seriousness in Aaron's voice. "Alright. I'll see a doctor. I wasn't trying to pick an argument, I just don't think it's a big deal. But since it bothers you this much, I'll do it. I'm sorry."

"Now, Jeannie," Aaron said, rising to his feet.

"What? Now?" Jeannie rose to her feet, too. "We were just having lunch."

"Lunch can wait."

"Oh, come on. At least let me finish the noodles before I get pricked with needles and scanned by machines."

"Jeannie…" Aaron took her hand. "You had breakfast, I'm sure you can put off lunch for a few hours and be alright. If I let you have your way, you'd rather not go. Now, come on. It won't take long. I promise."

Jeannie reluctantly obliged. If it was what Aaron wanted, then the least she could do was let him have his way. Plus, this way, she could spend more time with him while secretly enjoying the fact that he worried so much for her.

Twenty minutes later, they were both seated in Dr. Mendel's office waiting for the lab results. Aaron had walked out of Lily's hospital room holding Jeannie's hands tightly. Many of the nurses had seen, and a lot of them whispered to each other. Seeing how protective Aaron was of her caused tingles to form in her stomach. It didn't stop, even after thirty minutes had passed.

Jeannie hated needles, but she had to endure getting pricked twice to draw blood. They had checked her blood pressure, too, taken a swab of her saliva…urine…and a lot of other stuff. Jeannie didn't mind as long as Aaron was there with her, like her personal handbag.

"Why are you staring at me, Jeannie?" Aaron asked, snapping her out of her thoughts. "Are you nervous?"

Jeannie blinked repeatedly. She had not realized that her eyes had been on Aaron for so long. "No. I'm not nervous. I was just thinking deeply, that's all."

"Sorry for keeping you both waiting for so long," Dr. Mendel interrupted them as he walked into the room. "I was doing my evening rounds."

"It's no problem at all," Jeannie said. "We should thank you for making time to see us."

Dr. Mendel took his seat and turned to his laptop. "So, I see here that a nosebleed brought you in for tests, Miss Miller."

Jeannie glanced at Aaron and sighed. "I know, right? I kept telling Aaron that it wasn't a big deal, but he wasn't having it."

Dr. Mendel sat back. "Well, your results are back. Your bloodwork came back clean. Your urine, too. No anomalies there."

"You see? I told you," Jeannie whispered to Aaron. "For someone who claims that I worry too much, you fuss over nothing."

"Hang on," Dr. Mendel continued. "That's the good news."

Jeannie's heart skipped a beat. "There's...there's bad news?"

Dr. Mendel sighed. "Your blood pressure is high, Miss Miller. Dangerously high. One-fifty over ninety. That is almost as severe as Aaron's hypertension. He came here with a BP of one-sixty over a hundred. If your blood pressure isn't lowered soon, you are at substantial risk of a stroke or even heart disease. You need to take things slow, Miss Miller."

Jeannie scratched her nape, avoiding eye contact with Aaron. "I didn't even realize."

"Usually, HBP has no or mild symptoms. So it's

important you check it regularly to know where you stand. When was the last time you had it checked?”

“She doesn’t know the answer to that question, Dr. Mendel,” Aaron said in her stead. “Will she be placed on the same medications I’m on?”

Dr. Mendel nodded. “Yes. I will prescribe her drugs and the dosage. You need to take them regularly. You also need to start eating healthier and exercising. It’s important you move around more, maybe join a gym.”

“No wonder Aaron is so fit,” Jeannie joked and laughed awkwardly. She had expected a reaction from Aaron, but his glare caused her to choke on her laughter. “I’ll take your advice, Dr. Mendel.”

“Go home tonight, Miss Miller,” Dr. Mendel continued. “You need a good night’s rest to start. You can come back tomorrow. I assure you, if there is any change in Lily’s health, you’ll be the first to know, ideally.”

“What? I really don’t think—”

“You’re still going to argue with the doctor, Jeannie?” Aaron asked her. “Still?”

Jeannie swallowed her words and caressed his hand to calm him down. “I wasn’t arguing...why do you look so angry?”

Aaron lifted his eyebrows. “You really don’t know?”

“I know,” Jeannie mumbled and looked away. “I’ll go home for the night. Rest, take the medication, and be back here tomorrow.”

“Thank you, Dr. Mendel,” Aaron said, rising to his feet. “We’ll be on our way now. Let’s go, Jeannie.”

The last thing Jeannie wanted was an earful from Aaron, so she didn’t say a word while he led her out of the doctor’s office. They picked up her medication and proceeded to Lily’s room to get Jeannie’s things. Jeannie said goodbye to Lily, got into Aaron’s car, and was home within the hour.

Aaron had barely said five words to her since her diagnosis.

Even in her own home, Jeannie sat at the edge of the couch, watching Aaron walk up and down the house like he owned the place. It was a bit too much for him to be angry, but if he was only worried, then he wouldn't be giving her the silent treatment. Still, Jeannie wondered when the time would be right to ask him why he was so upset.

"I'm not upset," Aaron said, walking out of the bathroom.

Jeannie gasped, impressed that he'd answered her question without her even asking. "You look upset."

"I'm not," Aaron said. "I just don't like it when you don't take care of yourself. You don't listen. I've said this countless times. Is it a habit? Why do you even have such a bad habit? Same thing with Luka. You didn't care that he hurt you, or that his presence was affecting everything. You didn't care how he affected you as long as you were doing the 'right thing.' I know this might sound weird, but would it be a bit much to ask you to see a therapist?"

Jeannie rose to her feet. "Are you saying I'm mentally ill?"

"I'm saying you might be traumatized or something," Aaron said.

"I don't need a psychologist. All I ever needed was a change of space. That's why I moved here. But somehow, problems just keep following me around."

"Then talk to someone," Aaron said.

"I talk to you."

"Are you saying I'm your therapist?"

"You and Cathy, yes."

Aaron snorted and bit his lower lip. "It's not funny."

Jeannie stifled a smile. "It is. A little."

"You keep saying you're fine when you are clearly not. You have hypertension, Jeannie. If it wasn't detected now, only God knows what could have happened."

Jeannie walked over to his side and wrapped her arms around his waist. "I don't want you to worry, that's all. I know deep down that I'm not fine. But I just say I am so you don't skip work because of me. It's something you can do. It's something you've done before."

"And I've never complained," Aaron said. "This is what a relationship is like, Jeannie. You tell me how you really feel, and you don't sugarcoat things so I don't worry. If I don't worry about you, what else am I doing with my life? Don't keep things from me."

Jeannie placed her head on his chest. "I'm sorry."

Aaron stroked her back and played with her hair. "I ran the water for you. Go in, take a nice, long bath, and let's have dinner together."

Jeannie lifted her head and smiled sheepishly. "Thank you."

"You're welcome."

Aaron stayed back in the kitchen trying to whip up something for dinner while she made her way to the bedroom, took off her clothes, and got into a robe. As soon as she put a foot into the bathtub, Jeannie could vividly feel her body relaxing. The water was warm, just the way she liked it. Jeannie had missed the floral scent of her shower milk, and the feel and familiar smell of her bathroom. It felt as though she had been gone for ages.

She sat in the water with only her head above the water level with a fixed, relaxed smile on her face. Thinking about it, she could have made time to come home for a bath and a few hours of rest instead of staying permanently in the hospital.

The silence in the bathroom felt so serene. Jeannie shut her eyes and imagined herself in the middle of the ocean, floating. She felt herself drifting further and further…

# Chapter Seven

Jeannie woke up with a fright. She inhaled deeply and scanned the room, as if she were in danger. When she realized she was in her own bed, she mellowed and set her feet down on the ground. The sun was already out in the sky, but the windows were closed, so they trapped the harsh rays outside. Jeannie glanced at the clock and gasped, calculating how long she had slept. It had been over ten hours since they got back from the hospital. She had to go back.

"Wait..." Jeannie mumbled, scanning the room.

Something wasn't right. How was she in bed dressed in her nightgown when the last thing she recalled was falling asleep in the bathtub? Jeannie staggered to her feet and massaged her temple with her fingers. Jeannie nodded and continued to scan the room. She wasn't wrong. Last night, she had gone into the bathroom for a bath while Aaron was in the kitchen preparing dinner.

"Did I fall asleep?"

Jeannie covered her mouth to muffle another gasp at the realization. She not only fell asleep in the bathtub, Aaron must have had to carry her out of there. Naked.

"No..." she mumbled again.

That was a far fetch. Perhaps she got out of the bathtub herself, got dressed and ready for bed, but then just couldn't remember it. Jeannie recalled how tired she was the night before. It was possible that she merely forgot all the details.

Knotting her robe firmly around her waist, Jeannie made her way to the living room. It was already past nine in the morning, so she figured Aaron had probably left for work. However, to her present surprise, she found him seated on her couch watching television. Jeannie paused to get a good look at him before he noticed her. She had never seen him so relaxed before. He had a coffee mug in his hand, his shirt was unbuttoned down to the middle, and he had his arms around the couch in a laid-back position. His laptop was placed on the side of the couch, opened and in use. Jeannie figured he had been working since he woke up.

"I can see you, you know?" Aaron said without turning his head. "If you aren't planning to attack me from the side, then why don't you come over and say hello?"

Jeannie rolled her eyes and walked up to him. "Hello."

He smiled and lifted his gaze to meet hers. "Hello, Jeannie. Did you sleep well?"

"I slept incredibly well," she answered and crashed on the couch. Jeannie snuggled into his arms and leaned on his shoulders. "I didn't dream, or even wake up in the middle of the night. I just...slept. It was so nice."

Aaron caressed the side of her arm. "I'm glad. You gave me a mini heart attack last night. I thought you were dead or something."

Jeannie arched her eyebrows and tilted her head upward. "What do you mean?"

"Last night," Aaron explained. "You fell asleep in the bathtub. You were in there for so long, I knew something was wrong. Then, I called out to you about three times. No answer. I was worried, so I had to go in and check on you. I cannot explain it in words, but the fear I felt at that moment, seeing you unconscious in the bathtub, knew no bounds. But I calmed down when I confirmed you were only sleeping. Deeply. I carried you out of the bathtub, got you into your nightgown, and tucked you in."

Jeannie sat upright. Her cheeks and ears had grown bright red. "You should have just woken me up. Why did you have to go through all that stress?"

"You were sleeping very deeply, Jeannie," Aaron explained. "I tried to wake you up, but you slapped my hand away from your shoulders."

"I did?"

"Yes, ma'am. I had no choice but to carry you. Do you know how difficult it was to get you into your nightgown? You kept turning, and you refused to stay still."

Jeannie stared at her fingers. "Sorry, and thank you. I guess I was exhausted."

"You were," Aaron said. "But it's alright. It was kind of funny. I was tired, too, so I slept by your side and got up to prepare breakfast this morning. I also had some work to do, and I just finished the proposal I was working on and sent it."

"That's good," Jeannie said and leaned into his arms again. "You need to take a break, too. And no, I'm not talking about the break you take by spending time with me. I'm talking about a vacation. Somewhere far from here. Don't you think it's well-deserved?"

"We can take one together then. When you have the time. There's no rush."

Jeannie chuckled. "Do you have to include me in all of your plans?"

"I must," he answered. "It's a matter of my relaxation. I have to do it my way."

"True." Jeannie nodded. "Let me make us some breakfast. I'm starving."

"Oh, I already made toast and some scrambled eggs," Aaron told her. "I left the dish in the microwave. I already ate."

"Whoa. I must have been a hero in my past life."

Her statement caused Aaron to chuckle. "Just eat," he said to her. "You didn't have anything to eat all day yesterday."

"Thank you. Are you going to the sawmill today?"

"No," Aaron said, shaking his head. "I'm spending the day with Lily."

"Oh, really?" Jeannie voiced, excited. "Then we're spending the day together. I'll have breakfast quickly, shower, and get dressed so we can leave."

"No…" Aaron said and pulled Jeannie back to him. "I'm spending the day with Lily. You are going to spend the day here. At home. Knitting a sweater or binge-watching a series. You're not seeing Lily today. It's my turn."

Jeannie scoffed. "You're funny."

"I wasn't telling a joke. I'm being serious. You're not leaving this house today."

Jeannie's eyebrows furrowed when she sensed Aaron meant what he said. "Come on. You're asking me to go the entire day without seeing my daughter."

"You have seen her enough in the last two weeks. I'm travelling first thing tomorrow morning. I would like to spend today at the hospital before I leave. Can you let me do this, please?"

"Well, all the more reason we should be together today, since I won't be seeing you for a few days," Jeannie argued. "Plus, I don't want to be idle."

"That's why I suggested knitting Lily a sweater or watching television. There is a lot you can do in the space of twenty-four hours."

"I can do all of that in Lily's hospital room. I can knit there on my favorite sofa, and there's a television. I can binge-watch whatever I want there. There's really no difference."

"There is to me," Aaron said. "You're not leaving this house. You were just diagnosed with HBP. The least you can do is take today off. I'll be with Lily. If anything changes, I'll call you."

"Aaron, you've already done too much for me," Jeannie said. "I can't ask you to babysit my daughter at the hospital."

"I remember volunteering because I want to. I don't recall you asking."

"Still. I'll…" Jeannie stammered. "I'll get one of those small beds like you suggested. That way, I won't sleep on the sofa anymore."

"That wasn't even up for discussion. I already placed an order for the bed to be brought in two days. Regardless, stay home, Jeannie."

"What if Lily wakes up?"

"Then my handsome face will be the first thing she sees," Aaron said with a smirk on his face. "I hope she wakes up while I'm there. It will make it easier for me to become her favorite person. I'll tell her I have been the one sleeping at the hospital for two weeks while her mother is at home knitting."

Jeannie slapped his arm playfully. "Aaron!"

"I'm joking," he said. "But I'm serious about you staying at home. If you refuse, I'll tell Dr. Mendel about it and have him ban you from Lily's hospital room."

"He can't ban me," Jeannie retorted.

"Whatever," Aaron said.

Jeannie shifted in her seat and faced Aaron. She wasn't ready to back down. "How about we do it like this—"

"Remember the time you sided with your ex-husband over me?" Aaron asked. "Or when you yelled at me because I was trying to help you by opening your eyes to who Luka truly was. Or when I was so worried about you, I slumped at the sawmill, and I had to go to the hospital because of a spike in my BP. Or the time when—"

"Alright, fine," Jeannie said, backing down. "Goodness, you are petty."

Aaron ran his fingers through her hair. "Stay home," he repeated. "You can go back to the hospital tomorrow. I want you in your bed for at least ten more hours today."

"Yes, sir," Jeannie said. "You'll call me if there's any change?"

"Definitely. Now, go and eat breakfast while I take a shower. I should be on my way."

Jeannie nodded in response. She rose to her feet and made her way to the kitchen. It was only a day. Spending one day away from the hospital would not hurt. Deep down, Jeannie knew she needed the break. She was going to use the day to the fullest. Starting with breakfast, taking her medication, and then...more sleep.

*The following day...*

"Did you get there safe?"

The break had done Jeannie more good than she had expected. She had divided the day in such a way that she could do a lot with her time off. But contrary to how Jeannie had planned it, she had spent half of the day sleeping. She didn't pick up one knitting pin, or a book, or the TV remote...in fact, she spent the day in bed. When she woke up this morning to prepare for her return to the hospital, Jeannie felt as though a truckload of stress had dissipated from her body. It turned out that all she needed to get rid of her back ache was one good night's sleep.

"I did," Aaron answered. "I'm checked into my hotel

already and I just had a meeting with my team to prepare. How's Lily? Has there been any change since I left?"

Jeannie glanced at Lily on the bed and sighed. "None. But Dr. Mendel says her scans are normal and we just have to wait for a bit. But I'm hopeful. Since he says all we have to do is wait, we wait."

"Look who's being optimistic," Aaron teased. "Be strong, Jeannie, alright? Lily needs you to pull through this. Keep talking to her like you always do. Who knows? She might be listening."

"Dr. Mendel said she's probably not," Jeannie said. "But I still talk to her. I mean, it's just the two of us here in this room, so who else do I have to interact with?"

"Make sure to pay attention to your health, too," Aaron told her. "I'm sure Dr. Mendel has told you all the things you should do, and things you shouldn't do. Do as he says, alright?"

"Look who's talking. You ignore Dr. Mendel's words all the time and eat pizza almost every day."

"That doesn't mean you should, too. No eating pizza until I return, alright? We'll reduce take-outs, too. Thinking about it, we eat a lot of junk food."

"Right?" Jeannie answered. "It's because we don't have time to prepare home-cooked meals. But I'm going to try to change that. I'll start dropping by the bakery in the mornings, at least for thirty minutes. I'll stop by the market, too, and I'll cook. That way, I spend at least two to three hours outside the confines of the hospital room each day."

"Alright. I like the sound of that. Three hours of fresh air every day is a start. At least until Lily wakes up."

"Yeah. Everything will go back to normal by then," Jeannie mumbled. "I shouldn't take much of your time. I know you have a big meeting to prepare for, so I'll let you go. Call me when you're done with the meeting?"

"Definitely," he answered. "I'll talk to you later. Love you."

"Love you, too."

Jeannie placed the phone on her chest and laid down on the sofa. It was late in the afternoon. Jeannie fiddled with her phone, contemplating who to call next. It was a school night, so Cathy would be busy with the kids. She couldn't call Mason because of the time difference…Emily, too. Jeannie was sure that Sarah would accept the call no matter the time, but she didn't want to bother her. Sarah had a habit of sending Jeannie money every single time Jeannie called her. It made it appear that was always the reason for her calls.

Still, Jeannie placed a call to Sarah. She was bored out of her skin and needed someone to talk to. Plus, eventually, she had to inform the children of her hypertension.

A knock on the door startled Jeannie. She sat up and stared at it. If it was the doctor, or a nurse, or even Cathy, they would have walked in. But this person was waiting to be ushered in.

"Come in," Jeannie said.

Even before the door opened, Jeannie put two and two together and guessed who the visitor was. There was only one person who hadn't shown his face at the hospital since they had checked Lily into that room. One person who really liked to disappear when it was convenient for him.

"Luka."

"Hello, Jeannie," Luka greeted with a smile. He strolled into the room with his hands behind him. "Is this a hotel room, or a hospital room?"

"What do you want?" Jeannie asked, rising to her feet.

"What else? I came to see my child," Luka answered. He walked over to Lily's bedside and sat on the chair. "I came to see Lily. What's going on? Why hasn't she woken up yet?"

"Ask the doctors for answers to your questions," Jeannie retorted. "You've seen her, now leave."

"Leave?" Luka frowned. "I'd appreciate it if you could put our differences aside in this moment. I'm not here to see you, I came for Lily."

Jeannie picked at her fingers, trying to figure out what to say in response. She didn't want him there, but then she didn't have a valid reason to chase him away. Like it or not, Lily was his child, too, and he had a right to see her.

"Then see her quietly and leave," Jeannie said and took her seat.

Luka turned back to Lily and watched her. For the next few minutes, he stayed quiet, making Jeannie think he was telling the truth when he said he was only there for Lily. But then another minute went by, and he cleared his throat to speak.

"I see your guard dog is out of town."

Jeannie shut her eyes and inhaled deeply. "Luka, I really don't want to talk to you. You put me in terrible moods. I see you, and I want to jump off a cliff. Please, see Lily and leave."

"Do you think it's fair that your little boyfriend got to see Lily more than her actual father? He's been here almost every day, hasn't he?"

"Are you serious right now?" Jeannie asked, losing her patience.

"Do you think I don't know? I've been here almost every day, too, and I see him. He spends hours in here with you. You think that's fair? Just because we have our differences doesn't mean that you should stop me from seeing my child."

"Who is stopping you?" Jeannie asked, enraged. "You didn't show up once, Luka. Did you come here, and I chased you away? After the surgery, you chose not to come. Now you appear out of thin air and you're saying nonsense? There is something wrong with you."

"Did you not just ask me to leave five minutes ago?" Luka asked, rising to his feet, too. "I knew that was going to be your response if I came. Plus, you had your guard dog with you twenty-four hours a day. I mean, he's the one paying for this room, so he must have every right to be here, right?"

"Do not call him that," Jeannie demanded. "I think it's time you go. If you are going to keep talking to me, then leave. You've seen Lily, nothing has changed in the last five minutes. If she wakes up, I'll make sure you're informed. So leave."

"You're making a mistake, Jeannie," Luka said. "Lily might be upset right now, but her feelings will not change. She and I just need to talk things over. Can't you see that all I'm doing, I'm doing for her?"

"No, you're doing it for yourself. Luka, you derive pleasure in making my life a living hell. What would it take for you to leave me alone?"

"I know what I did to Lily sixteen years ago was terrible. That is why I'm here trying to make up for it. Trying to give her the family that she wants. All I want to do is make sure you're comfortable, Jeannie. That you never have to work again in your entire life. Can you let me do that for you? Jeannie, I love you and you know this. You just choose to hurt me because you know how much I care about you."

Jeannie scoffed and crossed her arms. "You are so pathetic that it's laughable."

Luka approached her but Jeannie was quick to retreat. "Jenny..."

"If you keep annoying me, I will ask that you are removed from this room," Jeannie said to him. She stared into his eyes and shook her head. "I think I do need a therapist. How in the world did I survive with you in my life for twenty-six years?"

"What is that supposed to mean?" Luka asked. "We survived on our burning love for each other. Do you think it's easy to stay married for almost three decades?"

"It's easy when the husband vanished for more than half of it," Jeannie answered. "Go and say goodbye to Lily and leave. Or I promise you, I swear it…I will get security to remove you from this room if you say one more word to me."

Reluctantly, Luka stepped back. "Fine. But we're not done with this. When Lily wakes up, we will all discuss this. You need to stop thinking of yourself for once, Jeannie, and do what's best for our family."

Jeannie rolled her eyes and sat back down on the sofa. She had promised herself not to ever engage Luka in a conversation again, but the man had his ways of bringing out the worst in her.

About an hour passed, and Luka was still there seated by Lily's side. Jeannie was growing impatient. He had stayed quiet, but his presence alone irked her.

"Luka, I think you have overstayed your welcome," Jeannie said and grabbed her blanket from the table. "It's late. I'd like to get some sleep. Please, shut the door on your way out."

Luka didn't respond. He didn't even turn to look at her. Jeannie figured that he might be waiting to start up another conversation when the heat of the last one had died down. She wasn't going to give him the opportunity.

Jeannie fluffed her pillow and laid down on the sofa. She covered her body with the blanket and shut her eyes. Perhaps if Luka saw that she was asleep, he'd have no choice but to leave. It was obvious that he didn't come to see Lily. He came in an attempt to get into Jeannie's head again.

Some time had passed…Jeannie wasn't sure how long, but sleep was starting to kick in. Her mind was starting to drift further and further away when something brought her back to reality. She could swear she felt breathing on her skin.

As she tried to open her eyes to scan her surroundings, Jeannie felt something cold press against her lips, followed by the scrape of a finger on her cheek. Her eyes flew wide open in an instant, and she struggled to sit up. Luka didn't back away. He took her lips into his and kissed her amidst Jeannie's struggling.

Finally, after what seemed like an eternity, Jeannie was able to push Luka off with all her might and send him tumbling over the table. She sprung to her feet, panting and red with rage. Jeannie wiped her lips with the back of her palm.

"Alright, Jenny. Calm down," Luka asked, staggering to his feet. "I acted on impulse. I'm sorry. I couldn't help myself."

Jeannie was about to scream, but they were in the coma ward. Screaming wasn't a good idea. The hospital could have them both kicked out.

"Get out!" Jeannie rasped, shaking with anger. "Out!"

"Would you let me explain?"

Jeannie moved to Luka's side and shoved him. She shoved him again and kept at it until they were at the door. Luka made to say something, but one last shove sent him to the ground outside the room. Jeannie slammed the door shut and guarded it with her body.

Luka had to disappear. He had to leave her life for good, else Jeannie feared he'd ruin everything all over again.

# Chapter Eight

"He kissed you?"

"Lower your voice, Cathy."

When Jeannie had phoned Cathy and asked her to come to the hospital first thing in the morning, Cathy had sensed something was wrong. So, after dropping the twins off at school, she came over to the hospital. Cathy's reaction to the news was just how Jeannie had imagined it. She let out a loud, dramatic gasp, covered her mouth, and rose to her feet.

"Sit down, Cathy," Jeannie asked.

"I cannot believe my ears," Cathy said and sat down. "The audacity. He actually kissed you?"

"Yes," Jeannie answered. "Cathy, you cannot even begin to imagine how disgusted and dirty I felt."

"Wait, like...what kind of kiss?" Cathy asked. "Like a grandma kiss? Or like a full on 'I want to devour you' kiss?"

"He tried to stick his tongue in my mouth, Cathy. If my lips weren't shut tightly, he would have succeeded."

"Oh my goodness!" Cathy yelled and rose to her feet again.

"I wasn't even there and I am disgusted. You need to do something about Luka, Jeannie."

"I know."

"He still thinks he has access to you and your body. He is delusional. To him, you both are just separated for the time being. I'm sure he thinks he can still have you back as his wife."

"I think it's time I stop looking at things from my perspective," Jeannie said. "I keep assuring everyone, including myself, that Luka and I are done. That bridge is burnt. But now I have to sit down and think about why Luka still thinks he can win my heart. What am I not doing to make it clear?"

"Exactly," Cathy said, sitting down. "If you want to beat a con artist, think like a con artist. He wants access to you. So, what do you do?"

"Cut it off."

"Yes," Cathy said.

Jeannie snapped her fingers. "I can report him. I mean, it's harassment. What he did is technically sexual harassment."

Cathy shook her head. "It is, but I don't think that will keep him at bay. A restraining order, on the other hand, is what Luka needs. He can see you from afar, but he cannot contact you in any way. That is how you cut it off."

Jeannie gasped softly. "That's right. A restraining order. I thought of it before, but it skipped my mind. It's perfect."

"You need Aaron's help to get it," Cathy said. "Well… technically, you don't because you can file for a restraining order yourself and represent yourself in court, but it will be more impacting if Aaron has something to do with it."

Jeannie moved closer to Cathy, intrigued by the conversation. "What do you mean?"

"Think about it. Who does Aaron hate the most in all of this? Who does he think is the reason you are so adamant on keeping him away?"

"Aaron."

"Correct, Aaron. Now imagine that Aaron was in court during the order hearing, and his lawyer represented you."

"It would be rubbing salt into Luka's injury. Like bruising his ego."

"Not to mention, Aaron's lawyer is one of the best in Chickadee Cove," Cathy continued. "I think that's even more reason you should ask Aaron. His lawyer will get you the restraining order with ease."

Jeannie fiddled with her fingers. "I don't know. Aaron is already doing so much for me, way more than I do for him. Don't you think it would be too much to ask him?"

"Do you want to get rid of Luka or not?"

"You know I do."

"Then talk to your boyfriend," Cathy said. "But don't tell him Luka kissed you."

"You think it's a bad idea, don't you?"

Jeannie had been racking her brain all night trying to figure out how Aaron would react to the news. He was bound to get angry. There was even the possibility of him attacking Luka. If that happened, then Luka was going to use it to his advantage. In fact, Jeannie was almost certain that Luka would be glad if Aaron threw the first punch so he could play the victim card again.

"I like what you and Aaron have going right now," Cathy continued. "If you tell him that your ex-husband visited you at night and kissed you, there are about two or three ways it could play out. For one, he wouldn't believe that it wasn't consensual. And you can't blame him. You've taken Luka's side twice in front of him. He could get angry, find Luka, beat him up, and get sued. That would be your fault, too, because if you had listened to us from the start and—"

"I know what you're driving at," Jeannie groaned. "But if I

don't tell Aaron about this, how do I ask him for help with the restraining order?"

"He knows you want Luka gone now, so I don't think you need to bring up the kiss for him to agree. He wants Luka gone, too, doesn't he?"

Jeannie dropped her shoulders. "Yes. I feel I should be honest with him, though."

"Right," Cathy said and shook her head. "Why did you even let Luka come into this room in the first place?"

"What should I have done? He lied and said he wanted to see Lily and not me. He sat there for over an hour looking at Lily, then the moment I put my guard down, he decided to give me nightmares. Cathy, Aaron and I are just getting back together. He is everything I want in the world, all wrapped up in one person."

"I know," Cathy told her. "Don't worry. I don't think getting a restraining order is going to be a hassle."

Jeannie nodded. "I don't think so, either."

A part of Jeannie wanted to tell Aaron about what Luka did. But a bigger part of her didn't want to see Aaron angry. Her only hope was that Aaron understood. Once she got the restraining order, everything was going to be normal again.

# Chapter Nine

"I brought lilies for Lily, and roses for you, my precious rose."

The day she dreaded had finally arrived. Aaron was standing in front of her with two bouquets of flowers in his hands and a bright smile on his face. Jeannie had stayed up all night thinking of different possible ways to tell him what Luka had done. None of them sounded good in her head, so she had gone with Cathy's plan. Lie.

Or rather...hide the truth.

"Thank you so much, Aaron," Jeannie beamed, taking the flowers from him. "Although, I'm not sure buying lilies for Lily was a good idea."

Aaron walked into the room and set the bags he'd brought with him down. "Why?"

"Well, the last time I recall someone buying Lily flowers was during junior prom," Jeannie explained. "The poor guy said the same thing. He bought lilies for Lily and she slammed the door in his face."

"Oh, she hates lilies?"

"I don't think she likes the cheesy line. Lily isn't a

romantic person," Jeannie explained. "That's why I'm looking forward to the man that will win her heart. He must have tough skin."

Aaron chuckled and sat by Jeannie's side. Instinctively, Jeannie moved away and in that instant, Jeannie bit her lip, realizing what she had done seemed suspicious. She treated secrets as though they were body odor. If Aaron was close enough, he could smell it.

"Are you alright?" Aaron asked, taking her hand. "You seem nervous."

"Nervous?" Jeannie tried to laugh it off. "I'm just glad you're back, that's all."

"Your hands are trembling," Aaron stated. "Are you sick?"

Before she could respond, he placed his palm on her forehead. "You don't feel warm. What is it?"

"Nothing," Jeannie said, taking her hand away. "I'm fine. Now, tell me about your trip."

"No," Aaron said and shook his head. "Tell me what it is right now."

"What...what it is?"

"What you're keeping from me."

Jeannie swallowed. She was dating a ghost...or maybe a psychic. Aaron seemed so sure she had a secret, and she was amazed at how quick he was to sense it. The best she could do to avoid telling him about Luka's actions was to bring up the restraining order. That was an obvious reason to explain why she was tense.

"I was just thinking of something, that's all," Jeannie answered.

"Thinking of what?" Aaron asked. "Is it about Lily?"

"No, not Lily. I want to get a restraining order," Jeannie announced. "For Luka. I just feel like it's the right thing to do, you know...to be sure."

Instead of Aaron's gaze softening, he stared at her with squinted eyes. "A restraining order?"

"Yes."

"Why?"

"Why? I mean, isn't it obvious? I don't want Luka around me. This is the only way I can make sure he's gone for good and never bothers me again."

"Why now?" Aaron asked. "What happened while I was gone? What changed your mind?"

Jeannie laughed awkwardly. "Aaron, nothing happened. Why do you look so serious? I just feel the need to get one, that's all."

Aaron stared at her and said nothing. He knew. Jeannie didn't know how, but he had figured it out. He might not know the specifics, but Aaron knew something was wrong, and if she kept denying it, he'd get angry.

"You're not buying it, are you?"

"Not even a little bit," he answered. "You make it so obvious that you're keeping something from me, and given your history of always hiding things, it's safe to say I can tell when you're doing it. Like right now. You've been fiddling with your fingers since I arrived, and you're seated at the edge of the sofa."

Jeannie opened her mouth to speak, but there was no excuse coming to her mind. She dropped her shoulders and shut her eyes tightly.

"Luka kissed me," she announced. "Three days ago. The day you arrived in Miami. He came and he kissed me when I was trying to get some sleep. He said he came to see Lily, but I should have known he had ulterior motives."

Patiently, Jeannie waited for Aaron to say something, but when he remained silent for too long, she slowly opened her eyes to look at him. He was on his feet now with his arms crossed.

"I'm sorry," Jeannie apologized. "I wasn't trying to hide it from you."

"Yes, you were. That's what you were just doing. You weren't going to tell me."

"For good reason."

"I'd like to hear that good reason," Aaron said. "Why would you keep this from me, Jeannie? I have told you more times than I can count to stop keeping things from me. Is it so difficult to trust me? I tell you everything."

"I know."

"Then why can't you do the same? I hate that I have to hassle you for information," Aaron said and started to pace. "It's like I'm a detective, and you're a criminal."

"A criminal?" Jeannie frowned.

"You know what I mean. I'm being serious, too," Aaron continued. "You are comfortable with lying to me and I don't like it. I really don't."

Jeannie rose to her feet and approached him. "I'm sorry. I didn't want you to get angry, that's all. We just started seeing each other again. I thought telling you about what Luka did would cause a fight between us."

"Why would we fight? Did you kiss him back?"

"What? Of course not," Jeannie said. "I kicked him out of the room immediately."

"Then we need to report him for harassment," Aaron said.

"No," Jeannie said, shaking her head. "Cathy said a restraining order is best. If I report him for sexual harassment, he'd only get a fine. I want to make it so that if he comes near me, he can get put in jail. A restraining order."

Aaron sighed. "So you told Cathy, but you couldn't tell me?"

"I'm sorry," Jeannie whined. "I only want to be in your good books. Forgive me, please? I know that something like this isn't going to happen again, so we have nothing to worry about."

Aaron sighed and ran his hand through his hair. "Alright. But in the future, if I ever have to hassle you for—"

"You won't," Jeannie assured him. "I'll tell you everything."

"Good. We'll go and see my lawyer in the morning. His name is Terry Franklin. He can help you get the restraining order."

"Thank you."

Aaron pulled Jeannie toward him and placed a kiss on her forehead. They hugged for the longest time, rocking back and forth. It was the last time she was ever going to have to hide something from him, and she was going to make sure of it. Once Luka was gone, Jeannie would have no reason to keep secrets.

<hr>

"Evidence?"

Terry Franklin was much younger than Jeannie thought he'd be. He was in his mid-thirties, with chestnut brown hair and sky-blue eyes. One look at the man and Jeannie could tell that she was in good hands. The man radiated confidence.

"Yes, evidence," Terry said.

Jeannie glanced at Aaron and then turned back to him. "I'm afraid I don't understand what you mean, Mr. Franklin."

They were seated in his office, a one-story building in the middle of Chickadee Cove. The man ran his own firm, Terry Franklin and Associates. Aaron claimed to have known him for years. Terry handled the legal aspects of Aaron's business.

"Please, call me Terry," he said and leaned on his table. "We are going to be working together now. I'd like us to have a comfortable relationship."

"Alright, then call me Jeannie, too," Jeannie answered. "What do you mean by evidence? I need proof to get a restraining order?"

"Yes, I'm afraid you do," Terry said. "There must be a reason you're filling for the order. You can testify in court, and it might suffice, but it's easier to have evidence to back up your claims."

"Well, I have a lot of evidence, but nothing physical," Jeannie said. "My testimony should be enough, I presume. I have twenty-six years' worth of evidence. My life is my evidence. Our divorce is my evidence."

"While that helps, it's much easier to have a...recent reason. You said he kissed you?"

Jeannie nodded in response.

"Against your will?"

"Yes. I was on my own. My eyes were closed, I didn't even see it coming."

"Good," Terry said. "That's our evidence. We just need him to confess to it."

Jeannie arched her brows. "Confess to it?"

"Yes, Jeannie," Terry said. "On record, that is. What I want you to do is call him and get him to talk about it."

Jeannie turned to Aaron and sighed. "I really don't like talking to him."

"Just until he makes the confession we need," Aaron said to Jeannie and took her hand. "Until he confesses. One last time. After this, you won't have to deal with Luka again."

Jeannie placed her other hand on Aaron's and braced herself. "Alright. If it will help me in the long run, then I am more than happy to endure listening to his voice."

"Good. I'll be recording, so just put it on speaker and talk casually," Terry said, reaching into his drawer.

Jeannie took out her phone from her bag and placed a call

to Luka. She held her breath as the line started to ring. Less than five seconds later, the call connected.

"Jeannie," Luka said. "Is something wrong? Did Lily wake up?"

"No," Jeannie said. She drew in a shuddery breath and placed the phone on the table. "I called because I cannot stop thinking about what you did to me. You took advantage of me, Luka. I was asleep, and you took advantage of it."

They heard Luka sigh. "Is that how you choose to see it?"

"How else am I supposed to see it?"

"Jeannie, I told you. I love you, and I couldn't help myself. My intention was never to harass you. Honestly speaking, I have been thinking about kissing you since the very first night I saw you when I arrived here in Chickadee Cove."

Jeannie exhaled in relief. Getting him to confess was a lot easier than she had expected it to be.

"Why won't you take no for an answer?"

"Because I know that sometimes, 'no' means 'maybe.' There is still hope for us, Jeannie. I have done so much to be with you. I even faked cancer, for heaven's sake. Can't you see that my intentions are pure?"

Jeannie glanced at Terry and he gave her a thumbs up, signaling that he had gotten what he needed.

"Goodbye, Luka."

"Wait, Jeannie. Okay, I'm sorry for kissing you without your consent, but are you going to lie to yourself that you felt nothing in that moment?"

"I'm not lying to myself. I felt something. Anger. I was angry. I wanted to strangle you in that moment for touching me. Goodbye, Luka."

With that, Jeannie ended the call. She knew that if she let Luka say another word, they were bound to start exchanging words with each other.

"Is it enough?" Jeannie asked. "Is it enough to keep him away from me?"

Terry smiled. "It's enough."

They talked more about the case and how everything was going to play out. Terry informed Jeannie that they were going to meet after he submitted the request to the court. He needed to prepare her for her testimony. All the while they talked, Jeannie's phone kept buzzing, nonstop. Luka didn't stop calling her. She knew talking to Luka was a terrible idea. He had seen an opening, and he probably thought he had a chance, since she reached out first. All of that was going to change soon.

# Chapter Ten

*A week later...*

The day of the trial had finally arrived. Jeannie had been wildly uncomfortable since the night before. She found it hard to go to sleep or think of anything else. The last time she had to get an attorney for anything was when she wanted to file for divorce. Jeannie recalled that moment vividly. She remembered how enraged Luka had been when the case was settled. The divorce process had been messy. It was one Jeannie did not want to relive ever again. Thankfully, Terry had assured her that restraining order hearings were different. Usually, smoother. It was all going to be concluded in a day.

Luka had been served the court papers last week. At least, that was what Terry had said. Jeannie was surprised that he hadn't shown up to confront her about it. The news must have come as a shock to him, yet he kept his distance. It made her wonder what he was thinking or planning.

Then again, knowing who Luka was, he was probably trying to call her bluff. Luka still held on firmly to the idea that Jeannie was in his grasp. Under his control. Or that she was just playing hard to get. She couldn't wait to use it to her advantage.

Aaron had been kind enough to pick her up that morning and take her to court. They had arrived shortly after and parked outside the building. Jeannie got out of Aaron's car and walked into the street. Although the sun was hot that morning, and its harsh rays made it difficult to keep her eyes open, Jeannie felt cold. She prayed to God that everything would go her way, at least this once.

For her outfit, Jeannie had gone for a black suit and pants with a blue camisole. She had tied her hair into a neat, high bun and wore only lip gloss as makeup. Once inside the courthouse, they made their way to a private room where lawyers met with their clients first before the court session began. Terry had asked them to meet him there so they could have a brief chat before they had to go in. They walked into the room and found Terry stationed by a shelf filled with books. He waved at them, then gestured to his phone slapped to his ear.

"Looks like he's on a call," Jeannie said to Aaron. "We're all here. That's good."

"Are you nervous?" Aaron asked Jeannie and took her hand. "You've barely said a word since this morning."

Jeannie tightened her grip on Aaron's hand and shook her head. "I'm not nervous."

"Jeannie...we talked about this," Aaron said, giving her a knowing look. "I'll ask again. Are you nervous?"

Jeannie bit her lower lip and nodded. "Very nervous, if I'm being honest. I don't know why. I mean, you hired one of the best attorneys in Chickadee Cove for this case. He has assured me countless times that everything will work out, but I just don't know why I can't calm down. My palms are sweaty, my heartbeat is through the roof, and I can only take short breaths."

"It's normal," Aaron told her. "We'll be out of here soon. There's absolutely no reason the judge would deny you this restraining order. I'll be there, and Terry will be there, too."

"I just...I read online that a testimony from a close friend helps cases like this a lot," Jeannie said. "Perhaps I should have asked Mason or Emily to be a witness?"

Aaron put his hands on Jeannie's shoulders and shook his head. "Terry said the evidence is more than enough to get the order. Trust him. Given the circumstances, what judge won't grant you your request? You're divorced from this man, the paperwork and messy suit is all there in the records. There's what Luka did to Lily, there's the fact that he's here in Chickadee Cove for no reason. Also, the fact that he lied about having cancer. It's obvious. The judge will see it, too."

"You think so?"

"Yes. I do. Now relax."

"Good morning, team," Terry beamed, joining them. "Sorry, I was on a call with my wife. She's angry 'cos I didn't inform her before leaving home this morning. On top of that, I didn't eat the dinner she set for me last night."

"You deserve her rage," Aaron told him. "She must have put a lot of effort into that meal for her to call you and complain."

"I know," Terry groaned. "I'll make it up to her somehow. Now, on to our case. You look good, Jeannie."

"I do?" Jeannie asked, concerned. "Is that good or bad? I don't want it to affect the case. I mean, the judge might—"

"Forgive her," Aaron cut in. "She is just nervous."

Terry chuckled. "It's normal to be nervous. It doesn't matter, Jeannie. You look good. Your appearance isn't what the judge is after. He just needs to look at the evidence and we're golden. Trust me. We will be in and out of here within two hours."

Jeannie sighed in relief and nodded. "Thank you. I'm

sorry. I trust you. Let's get Luka out of my life for good this time."

"I'm glad I'll be able to help with that," Terry said. "So, it's simple. When the judge walks in, we all rise. He'll call out the case, ask if we are all present, and ask us to proceed. You know Luka, do you think he'll come with a lawyer for dramatics?"

"I highly doubt it," Jeannie said. "He might not even show up."

"Well, if he doesn't, then that's good for us. It makes it easier without his objections and interruptions, and the judge will grant the order in no time."

"If he does show up, I don't think he'll come with a lawyer," Jeannie continued. "Luka is full of himself."

"Either way, we have this in the bag. Just do as I say and we're good. Alright?"

"Thank you, Terry," Jeannie said. "And thank you, Aaron. I love you so much."

"I love you, too," Aaron said and planted a kiss on her lips. "We're going to be fine."

"We are."

A few minutes later, they walked out of the room and into the courtroom. Jeannie's breath caught in her throat when she saw Luka seated already, waiting. She scoffed, relieved and amused that he came. Hopefully, this was the last time she saw him.

"All rise."

It was time. Jeannie sat on the left side of the courtroom with Terry by her side and Aaron in the audience. Luka was alone. He sat on the other side dressed in an expensive white suit, his beard neatly trimmed.

"Thank you, you may all be seated," the judge said. She was a middle-aged, tall, lanky woman with a pixie cut. "We are here today for docket number 2o21-90-1021. This is a case of

Miss Miller versus Mr. Smith, and it is for an order of protection.”

“An order of protection?” Jeannie whispered to Terry.

“It’s the same thing,” he whispered back.

“Are both parties present?” the judge asked.

“Yes, your honor,” Terry answered as they all took their seat.

“Good, we may proceed.”

They began the hearing with Jeannie’s testimony, and once Terry started talking and presenting evidence, an hour flew by. Luka kept denying everything Jeannie said, right down to the evidence. He claimed it was forged. He asked the judge not to let such an order tarnish his image. Luka even tried to use Lily to his advantage.

“Your honor, I have a daughter in the hospital,” Luka pleaded. “Does it make any sense that her mother thinks this restraining order hearing is of more importance than our daughter’s health? Sure, I made mistakes in the past. I admit to it. I left her countless times, but I promise I had reasons. I never hit her or abused her. She’s sitting there, you can ask her yourself. Not once did I touch her. Right now, I just want to be with my daughter, and this is preventing me from doing so. Jeannie might hide under the guise that I am supposedly a threat to her and her mental health, but I don’t think it matters now. I just want to be with my daughter, and I am afraid that if this restraining order is served, I won’t be able to be. Lily loves me, and Jeannie is jealous of this.”

“Your honor, we’d like to present evidence regarding Lily Smith, the daughter in question. We have reasons to believe that Luka’s absence in her life would be greatly beneficial to the young lady. Starting with the fact that he was the reason she was kidnapped sixteen years ago in the first place. She got into an accident on the fifth of this month because he brought her to Chickadee Cove. He is the reason she’s lying in that hospital bed, fighting for her life. This all boils down to the fact that he was trying to manipulate my client by lying about his health to get close to her again. I mean, your honor, we can hear it in that recording. He said it himself. He came to Chickadee Cove for the sole purpose of getting Jeannie back, and my client constantly refuses his gestures, but he won't leave her alone. This order of protection is paramount for my client's peace of mind, your honor."

The hearing went on for another hour until it was finally time for the judge to pass judgment. With her heart in her mouth, Jeannie rose to her feet.

"Based on the evidence presented to me today, including the testimony of the plaintiff," the judge started, "I do find that Miss Meadow's testimony is credible and that she has met the burden of proof for me to grant this protection. This order of protection will be in effect for three years, after which you, Miss Miller, will need to renew. Do we have any questions from both parties?"

"No questions on our part, your honor," Terry answered.

"What about on your part, Mr. Smith?"

Luka scoffed and clenched his jaw. "None, your honor."

"Thank you, and good luck to you both."

"Thank you, your honor."

If they weren't in court, Jeannie would have leaped for joy. Finally. Some peace and quiet in her life.

<hr>

"Yes, Cathy. It's valid for three years, and if Luka breaks it, he'll be arrested."

Her excitement knew no bounds. It was a long-awaited victory. Luka was finally down from his high horse, and it was now clear to him that they were over. Jeannie had to be at the hospital with Lily all the time as her legal guardian; therefore,

Luka couldn't use her as an excuse to be in the same room with Jeannie. If he wanted to see Lily, he had to make it known beforehand so Jeannie wouldn't be there. Whatever happened, it was impossible for Luka to see her or have access to her.

"I am so relieved, Jeannie," Cathy said over the phone. "Honestly, seeing Luka did things to me. I got angry all the time, irritated…I mean, I'm so happy for you, Jeannie. You finally did it. You finally cut the cord."

"It's the first step toward many changes that are to come. I'm going to be better, Cathy. With Luka finally out of my life, I feel a hundred times lighter than before."

Cathy sucked in through her teeth. "But do you really think he'll honor the restraining order? We both know Luka, Jeannie. He is a difficult, persistently annoying man."

"And he's very proud, too, so this is going to leave a dent in his ego," Jeannie said. "But I also know that he doesn't want to go to jail. To avoid that, he has to leave me alone. He should be glad I didn't sue him for harassment. I'm sure Aaron's lawyer Terry would have won that case, too, if I had. But I just want him away from me. I don't want any form of compensation or anything like that. I just want Luka gone. And I've got that. So, all that's left is to focus on Lily and my life."

"Like I said, I'm happy for you. I'm sure now, Aaron knows that you're serious about your relationship with him."

"Right?" Jeannie shrieked. "With this, I just proved to him that I'm capable of sorting out my feelings. I'm pretty sure deep down, he was doubting me, but now, he has no reason to."

"Speaking of Aaron, where is he?"

"He went to get us something to eat," Jeannie answered. "We're back at the hospital. The nurse just changed Lily's IV bag for the night. Aaron and I are going to sleep here in the hospital, then we'll go home in the morning to freshen up."

"Why didn't you just go home tonight?"

"I don't know…I guess I wanted to stay with Lily. Cathy, it's been almost a month. I am numb. If Lily doesn't wake up soon, I have no idea what I'm going to do."

"Speak to the doctor tomorrow and hear what he says," Cathy suggested. "I'm pretty sure they would be thinking of a solution to this, too. We have to believe that things will turn out fine."

"I know," Jeannie said, massaging Lily's arm with her hand. "I just need it to happen a little bit faster."

"You thought you got rid of me, right?"

Jeannie gasped so loud that her body jerked in shock. She spun around, and the phone slipped and dropped to the floor as her eyes fell on Luka. He looked untidy, different from how he had looked in court. His tie was loosened, his hair looked unkempt, and his jacked was missing.

"I have a restraining order," Jeannie said, trying to maintain her composure. She was scared that if Luka sensed her fear, he would take advantage of it.

"And you thought that was going to stop me?" he questioned, walking into the room stealthily. "How dare you, Jeannie? How dare you try to make a fool of me?"

"You brought this on yourself. I can't believe that even after all you did to me, you still have the audacity to come here and confront me like you did nothing wrong."

"Why couldn't you be civilized?" Luka rasped. "Did you really have to involve the law? Did you, Jeannie?"

To Jeannie's relief, Aaron walked in through the door. He said nothing at first and only glanced at Luka, then at Jeannie. He strolled into the room holding a bag in his hand. He stood in front of Luka, so close that their faces were only inches apart.

"You must really want to go to jail," Aaron rasped. "Because I'm dying to put you there. How dare you come here?"

Luka stepped back and began to laugh. "Of course, you have your bodyguard protecting you. Have I ever done anything to hurt you, Jeannie, that you treat me like I'm some peasant?"

"Luka, the things you did to me hurt far worse than any physical beating would," Jeannie told him. "I wish I never met you. My life would have been so different. Do you know how many times I was harassed because of you? How much bullying my children had to endure because of you? The shame of you sleeping around? Sleeping with Mason's teacher? Your lies, your deception, your scams. You had money, Luka. You still do, yet you took from me. If I could go back in time, I would change it all. All of it. I wouldn't leave anything to chance."

"How could you even say that?" Luka roared. "After everything I've done for you!"

"You're screaming," Aaron told him. "If you don't leave now, I'm calling the police."

"I'm already doing that," Jeannie said and picked up her phone. She dialed the number while Aaron engaged Luka in a heated conversation.

"You really want my leftovers so badly that you are prepared to fight for it?" Luka said to Aaron in a bid to agitate him. "What do you even see in Jeannie that has gotten you so enchanted?"

"Probably the same thing that has you fighting for her attention right now," Aaron said. "Are you a child, Luka Smith? What's with the tantrum? You're like a toddler begging for mummy's attention."

Luka squared up to Aaron and clenched his fist. "Now, you listen here—"

"I wouldn't do that if I were you," Aaron said, cutting him off. "You're not sick, remember? On top of that, you have a restraining order filed against you. Don't you see where this is going? If I hit you, it's self-defense. Or I could just say I was protecting Jeannie. So if I were you, I'd unclench that fist and walk away."

"The police are on their way," Jeannie announced. "Need I remind you, Luka, that the station isn't far from here. I told them where we are. They'll be here in two minutes."

"Do I look like I care?" Luka asked, raising his eyebrows. "You are so ungrateful, Jeannie. After everything I've done for you. After all these years. Twenty-six years of my life! And this is what I get? A restraining order? You did this to me?"

"You did it to yourself," Jeannie said.

Luka started to approach her when the door was pushed open and two officers in uniform walked in.

"Oh, thank God," Jeannie sighed. "Officers, I was the one that made the call. That's him. He's the one disobeying a restraining order. He barged in here in a rage screaming at us."

One of the officers approached Luka and pulled out a set of handcuffs. Luka refused to oblige at first, but when the officer kept pulling his arm, he submitted. They handcuffed him and practically dragged him out of the room. Once he was gone, Jeannie slumped on the sofa.

"Are you alright?" Aaron asked, rushing to her side.

Jeannie paused to take in a deep breath. "No, I'm not. But I will be."

She had not imagined that Luka would defy the court order and approach her. But he did, and now, it was a cause for concern. If he was released by the police, then there was no telling whether he'd stay away for good.

A soft groan came from Lily's bedside. Jeannie lifted her head in time to see Lily softly twist in bed. She groaned loudly and licked her lips lazily.

"Lily..." Jeannie said and approached the bed. "Lily, are you awake?"

As if on cue, two nurses and a resident doctor rushed into the room with their test equipment. Jeannie stepped aside as they checked Lily's body from head to toe.

"She's awake," the doctor said. "Congratulations."

## Chapter Eleven

*ays later...*

D Jeannie was certain that if she took another step, she'd collapse on the floor and pass out. Her legs were on fire, her entire body was covered in sweat, and she could barely hold a breath. It felt as though she had been running for ages. Jeannie's mouth had grown completely dry, and for a moment she was terrified by how fast her heart was pounding.

"Enough, please. I might just lose consciousness at any minute," she breathed.

The baffling thing about Jeannie's situation was that anyone who walked by would think she was exaggerating. She had gone on the run with Aaron, and Aaron, on the other hand, looked completely unfazed. He wasn't even panting, neither was there a drop of sweat on his body. And they had been jogging together the entire time.

"When was the last time you went jogging?" Aaron asked, bringing both hands to his hips.

"Jogging?" Jeannie asked, still panting. "I'd have to think about that. Probably before I gave birth to Lily."

Aaron lifted his eyebrows. "Well, you look fit, so you must have been doing some exercise, right?"

"Not at all," Jeannie said and exhaled loudly. "I just look fit, I'm not nearly. I don't run unless something's chasing me."

Aaron chuckled and shook his head. "Well, now you must. You need to take care of your health, Jeannie. Now more than ever."

"Look who's talking," she answered.

Aaron gave her a knowing look and Jeannie laughed, instantly getting the message. Who better to advise her on fitness than a man who looked like he was carefully hand-sculpted on a Sunday?

"Fine," Jeannie said, shaking her foot to loosen it a bit. "But I'm not jogging every day. We'll do it once a week."

"No." Aaron shook his head. "Five times a week. You'll have your weekends off."

"Oh, there's no way I'm jogging five times a week," Jeannie countered. "Two times a week."

"Alright, four times a week."

"No. Three. Meet me in the middle," Jeannie said. "And it's only for thirty minutes. I still have a bakery to run and a child to care for after all."

"Alright then," he answered. "By the way, how is Lily? Is she still not speaking to you?"

Jeannie sighed. "She's not speaking to anyone."

It had been over a week since Lily had been discharged from the hospital. Jeannie recalled how overjoyed she had been when the doctor had told her after so many tests that there was nothing wrong with Lily. They had prescribed some medication and discharged her. But after Lily got home, she refused to talk. She only nodded, shook her head, and covered her head with a blanket when Jeannie asked her to say something. At first, Jeannie worried that Lily was somehow still traumatized by the accident and she needed help, but there was no way of confirming when Lily refused to tell them what exactly happened.

"She'll come around," Aaron said. "I'm sorry, Jeannie. I would help, but I don't know how to. Plus, I don't think Lily likes me very much, so it's best that I don't interfere. The last thing I want is to give her a reason to hate me. Girls her age don't like being told what to do."

"It's alright," Jeannie answered. "She'll come around, like you said. I just want to make sure there's nothing wrong with her, you know? I want to know what happened that night, how she got into the crash, how she's feeling, if she has nightmares...I just want to be sure she's fine. I know the doctors said she's alright, but..."

"I understand," Aaron said. "It'll feel better to hear Lily say it herself."

"Yes," Jeannie whispered. "She refuses to step out of her room, she barely touches her food...I don't know what's wrong with her, Aaron. I mean, I understand that she was in an accident, and she still might be traumatized by it, but I didn't expect her to completely shut me out."

"She's not shutting you out," Aaron said, pulling Jeannie into an embrace.

"Yes, she is."

"No, she's not," Aaron argued. "She just needs her space right now. I know it's difficult, but you need to respect it. When she wants to, she will come around herself. Just give her some time. Remember right before the accident, you destroyed the truth she had believed in. All her life, Lily adored Luka. Then she came to find out the mistake he made sixteen years ago that, in turn, reshaped her life somehow. It's a lot to take in. Before now, Lily thought you all hated Luka because he was an on-and-off father. Now, it turns out that much of that hate was because of her. Specifically what Luka did to her. I mean, come on. Give her a moment."

Jeannie leaned into Aaron's arms. "You're right. Why didn't I think of it like that? Lily must still be upset about what I told her about her father. I should give her time."

"You should. She'll come around," Aaron told her. "Who's with her right now?"

"Cathy," Jeannie answered. "I asked her to help me look after her this morning, so she's currently at the house. We should be getting back. Cathy has other things to do, and it'll be unfair to keep her."

"Alright, that's enough exercise for today. We'll pick up from where we left off tomorrow. Same time."

Jeannie took Aaron's hand, and they began to stroll back down the road. "Do you really wake up at 4 a.m. every morning?"

"Well, not every morning," he answered. "I'm not a machine, Jeannie. But I do like waking up early on most days. You'd be surprised by how much you can achieve when you wake up earlier than you're used to."

"Well, I think I've had enough surprises to last me for the rest of the year."

They both chuckled as they made their way back to the house. As much as she hated to admit it, she felt much better after the run. Her body felt lighter, and her head felt less stuffy. Like she could hear her own thoughts. Aaron had spent days trying to convince her to go on a run with him, and Jeannie feared she'd embarrass herself, being so out of shape. Although she managed to do just that, the run was good for her, and she looked forward to the next one.

Anything to spend more time with Aaron.

---

Jeannie placed her plate of mashed potatoes and green beans down on the table and sat. She picked up her phone and stared at the screen. Usually, at this time of the day, she would have at least gotten a call from one of her other three children. Ever since Lily got out of the hospital, they had made it a routine to call every day and ask how Lily was faring. Jeannie always made sure to set aside at least thirty minutes out of her day to receive their calls.

"That's strange," she mumbled.

One good outcome from Lily's discharge from the hospital was that Lily had gotten closer to her siblings. Or at least, that's what Jeannie thought. Normally, Emily, Mason, and Sarah had bickered with Lily. They could never find common ground, and Lily had the talent of getting on their nerves. But over the last few days, Emily, Mason, and Sarah had spent most of the calls trying to get Lily out of bed. They hadn't succeeded yet, but seeing the effort warmed Jeannie's heart.

Jeannie set her phone down on the table, guessing that her kids were probably too busy with their lives. She figured it'd be best to let them call at their own time. Mason, for one, was almost always practicing, and Jeannie hated to disturb him. Emily was either preparing lecture notes or giving a lecture, and Sarah, well...Sarah was the one person Jeannie could call anytime.

A knock on the door diverted Jeannie's attention from the food. She set her plate down and instantly rose to her feet to check who the visitor was. She wasn't expecting anyone. Cathy was at the hospital with her son, and Aaron was working that night.

Jeannie gasped at the realization and halted in her tracks. If it wasn't Cathy, and it wasn't Aaron, then it had to be Luka. Who else would be visiting her?

"Who's there?" she asked, hesitating to touch the door.

No response. Her suspicion was growing. Jeannie immediately scurried to the table and grabbed her phone. She dialed 911 and clutched the phone to her chest as she approached the door again.

"Who is at the door?"

"Mum, it's me...Sarah."

"What?"

Instinctively, Jeannie reached for the lock and slid it off then proceeded to open the door. Lo and behold, Sarah was at the door dressed like she had just come from the beach, with her beach hat and flared, two-step flower gown. Jeannie could hardly believe her eyes.

"How in the world..." Jeannie mumbled. "Sarah!"

Overjoyed, Jeannie practically leaped into Sarah's arms and swayed her from side to side, chuckling. She squeezed tight, intoxicated by the pleasant scent of her daughter's skin. It had only been months since they had physically seen each other, but to Jeannie, it felt like decades. When she had moved to Chickadee Cove, Jeannie had feared that it would be years before she saw her children again. But there Sarah was, in her arms.

"Oh, my sweet baby."

Sarah broke the hug and cupped Jeannie's face. "Am I drunk, or did you age backwards, mum?"

Jeannie chuckled and playfully smacked Sarah's arm. "Come in, my dear. Where are your bags? Did you travel with only a small handbag?"

"No, it's at the hotel," Sarah answered, not taking a foot forward. She remained in the same spot even as Jeannie gestured for her to come inside.

"The hotel?" Jeannie asked. "Why would you stay at a hotel?"

"Because I'm not alone, and you only have one spare room, which I assume Lily's staying in," Sarah said.

Jeannie squinted her eyes, noticing that Sarah was acting suspicious. "Sarah, what's wrong?"

A head popped out from the side, startling Jeannie. "She's just very terrible at pretending."

Another head popped out from the other side with a wide grin plastered on her face. "Hi, mum."

Jeannie's body froze, but her hands couldn't stop shaking. She was so excited, it was difficult to contain it. "Emily! Mason! Oh, heavens! Am I dreaming?"

Emily and Mason emerged from hiding and covered Jeannie in a warm hug. It seemed as though they had grown taller over the past couple of months. Jeannie barely reached their shoulders. Still, she wrapped her hands around their waists and jumped excitedly. There were scarcely any words to describe what she was feeling in that moment. All her children were there, in Chickadee Cove, in her home.

"Oh," Jeannie said with a quivering voice as she started to shed tears of joy. The more tears she wiped from her cheeks, the more tears fell. She cried, feeling an overwhelming sense of peace.

"Oh, don't cry, mum," Sarah said, joining their circle. "We didn't come here to make you cry. That wasn't the point of the surprise."

"It's tears of joy," Jeannie sniffed, trying to smile. "I'm so happy right now, you can't even imagine. I only dreamt of this happening. I didn't think I could ever get the four of you here in Chickadee Cove. I just can't believe it."

"Well, we came to see you, and Lily, and hopefully, cheer you both up," Emily answered. "You said Lily had been having a hard time opening up. Well, we're here to help."

Jeannie could hear Emily perfectly, but it was difficult to understand all she was saying with her head in the clouds. Emily had put on some weight. She could tell. Her face glowed, although she still had eyebags. Jeannie touched Emily's cheeks and caressed them.

Mason looked the same. He was always fit. Sarah, too.

Jeannie wondered how Sarah managed to maintain the same figure since she was eighteen. She had not changed a bit, except for the obvious glow that came from her wonderful honeymoon.

"Come in," Jeannie said, stepping into the room. "I was just having mashed potatoes for dinner. If I knew you all were coming, I would have made more."

"There's no need, mum. We already ate on the plane," Emily said, crashing on the couch.

"Oh, nonsense. I'll make you all some dinner right now," Jeannie said, clearing her plates. "Perhaps Lily will join us if she sees you all here. She's going to be so shocked."

"I like this house, mum," Sarah said, prancing around the living room. "It's cozy. Feels like an actual home."

Jeannie was about to respond when she heard a door creak. She paused, familiar with the faint creaking sound of Lily's bedroom door. As she turned to check, Jeannie caught Lily standing in the hallway dressed in a white free-flowing gown, with her hair partly covering her face. If she wasn't sure that it was her daughter, Jeannie might have passed out thinking it was a ghost.

"Lily!" Jeannie said and gasped. It was the first time Lily had stepped foot in the living room since they'd returned from the hospital.

Lily slowly scanned the room that she had made dead silent with her presence. "Don't tell me..." she said with a cracked voice. "Don't tell me you all came all this way because of me?"

Emily rose to her feet and approached Lily. "Is that the right way to welcome your sister you haven't seen in months?"

"The last time I saw you was at my wedding," Sarah said. "Mum said you didn't look too well but seeing you now...you look like a train wreck. Fresh out of the mental hospital."

"Sarah!" Jeannie cautioned her. "That's no way to talk to your sister. She's been through a lot."

Sarah mouthed the word 'sorry,' then turned back to Lily. "How are you feeling? Why aren't you speaking to mum?"

"I have nothing to say," Lily answered. "And if you all came because of me, then you wasted your time. I'm fine. I just need some alone time, that's all."

"Well, alone time is over," Mason said. "You have a knack for worrying your family, do you know that? We've been worried sick about you. The least you could have done is talk to us when we video called you. Now we're here, and you don't even seem the least bit happy to see us. How's that fair?"

Lily glanced at Jeannie and then stared at the ground. "Sorry," she said faintly. "But I'm fine. There was no need to come."

"Tell us that over dinner," Emily said.

"I'm not hungry," Lily said.

"Right," Mason said and approached Lily. He stopped in front of her and pointed to the dining table. "Go and sit. We're having dinner and you're going to use your words and tell us how you really feel."

"And you're not allowed to use the words 'fine' or 'okay' during dinner, alright?" Sarah told her, bringing both hands to her hips. "Now, go and sit, or I won't give you the bags I brought from Italy for you."

Lily lifted her head, higher than necessary, pushed her hair out of her face, and walked to the dining table. Jeannie watched her and scoffed. If she had known sooner that bickering with her siblings was all Lily needed to get up from bed, Jeannie would have begged them to come sooner.

# Chapter Twelve

"I'm telling you, it's hard. I need a break."

Jeannie couldn't recall the last time she had sat in the same living room with all her children, talking and laughing about anything and everything. If she had to guess, she'd say it was two years ago when they last laughed that loud. It was right before Luka reentered their lives. Right before the messy divorce process began. Jeannie hadn't realized just how much she had missed their talks until she got to experience them again.

"Sarah, please don't tell me you're seriously complaining about how difficult your vacation is," Mason asked, sitting up on the couch. "You're complaining about travelling? Really?"

"It's difficult, I'm serious," Sarah groaned. "I'm constantly jetlagged, it's difficult adjusting to time zones, and I have to be mindful of what I eat every time because I have a sensitive stomach."

"Sarah, just stop talking," Emily said. She sat next to Jeannie on the couch and had her head on Jeannie's shoulder. "Do you know what I would give to be you right now?"

"I'll literally sell my arm to live your life," Lily chimed in. "Not the married part. Just the 'waking up in a different city every day' part. I've never been on a decent vacation."

"I practically live on the football field," Mason said. "The season just ended, but we're back on the training field again. That's why when Emily suggested this visit, I jumped right on it. Even though it's just for a few days, coming here was worth it. This feels like a vacation to me."

"Me, too," Emily added. "I have to stare at books all day. I'm constantly doing research, lecturing, grading...sometimes it gets tiring."

"No one asked you to be so smart," Lily said. "You chose that path yourself. Some of us don't have a choice, you know?"

"Someone like who?" Emily asked. "Because it's definitely not you, Lily. You have options, but somehow, you just love to choose the strangest ones. You could live here with mum, but you refuse. You could go to school, get an actual degree and increase your chances of getting a decent job, but you refuse."

"She's young," Sarah said. "Let her be, Emily. Sooner or later, she'll realize what's best for her."

"That's if it isn't too late then," Mason said. "But you do you, Lily."

A knock on the door interrupted their conversation. "I'll get it," Mason said, rising to his feet.

Secretly, Jeannie hoped it was Aaron. She was dying to see the look on Mason's face when he met Aaron for the first time. Jeannie had told Aaron that her children had arrived before she went to bed the day before, and he had been excited about it. But it turned out that Aaron had an important meeting with his stakeholders that morning. Jeannie still hadn't heard from him, but she knew he was either going to call, text, or stop by when he was done.

"Some audacity you have, Luka."

"Luka?" Jeannie blurted and rose from the couch. She immediately hurried to the door to find Luka standing in the doorway with flowers in his hand.

Jeannie scoffed, unable to believe her eyes. "You really are enthusiastic about going to jail, aren't you, Luka? Or do you not know what a court order is?"

"Good evening, Jeannie," Luka said.

"It's really not a good evening," she answered. "You are breaking the law again and I will not hesitate to call the police if you don't leave my house right this second."

Jeannie wondered how Luka had found out the children were in town. She had hoped to God that morning that he wasn't aware. The last thing she wanted was for Luka to try his corny tactics on them. She wasn't going to stand by and allow him to twist his way into their minds like he had done with Lily.

"I'm not here for you, Jeannie," Luka said.

Mason crossed his arms defensively. "Who are you here for then?" he asked. "Because it definitely cannot be for us."

"I called him."

Jeannie and Mason turned simultaneously to find all three of her daughters standing behind them. It was Lily's voice, the one that admitted to calling Luka. Jeannie stared at Lily trying to read her face, but she came up with nothing.

"What were you thinking, Lily?" Mason asked, taking the words right out of Jeannie's mouth. "Why ruin everyone's mood this way?"

"I wasn't trying to ruin anyone's mood," Lily said. "I only wanted to speak to him."

"About what?" Emily asked. "What could you possibly have to say to him?"

"Lily, please don't tell us you have easily dismissed what we told you about the kidnapping incident sixteen years ago,"

Sarah said. "You cannot be that naïve. What could you possibly have to say to him?"

"And why didn't you tell anyone that you called him here?" Emily questioned. "Why did you keep it to yourself?"

"Calm down," Jeannie voiced. "If Lily wants to talk to him, then she can do just that behind my back."

"Lily, I'm really sorry I didn't visit you sooner," Luka said. "It's just...your mother got a restraining order against me, making it difficult to get to you. The last time I held your hands was that night when I pulled you out of the wrecked car. Apparently, getting a court order was more important to Jeannie than staying by your side."

"Watch what you say, Luka," Jeannie cautioned.

This wasn't the way she wanted to tell Lily about the restraining order. Jeannie had been skeptical about how well Lily would take the news. There was no telling how she would react, given that Lily really cared for her father despite his shortcomings.

"How could you, mum?" Lily asked. "Really? Now? You had to get the order against him while I was lying in the hospital fighting for my life?"

"You are damn right she had to," Mason said. "Mum, I'm glad you did. It was high time."

"What changed your mind?" Sarah asked.

There was no need telling them what the last straw that broke the camel's back was. Jeannie figured Mason might throw a punch, Emily might throw another, and Sarah might just claw Luka's eyes out. But Lily, on the other hand, wouldn't see why Luka kissing Jeannie was a big deal. She of all people was an avid supporter of their reunion.

"I got fed up," Jeannie answered, staring Luka down. "I was tired of seeing his face and letting him have access to me. So, I decided to do something about it. This had nothing to do with you, Lily. I was thinking of my sanity, and so I acted as I saw fit. I don't want Luka anywhere near me."

"Tell him what you want to so he can leave, Lily," Mason said.

"That is no way to greet your father, Mason," Luka said. "You are my only son. Is it too much to expect a little trust and respect from you? I may not be a husband to your mother anymore, but you cannot change the fact that I am still your father. No matter what you do, that is what I will remain. That goes for you, too, Emily and Sarah. How about you kids let your mother and I have our differences? It seems as though you are inheriting her hatred for me, and it's not fair."

Emily shook her head pitifully. "You think we inherited it?"

"We were directly affected," Sarah added.

Mason took a step back. "On our way here, my sisters and I promised ourselves that we wouldn't get into a quarrel with you if we happened to run into you. We came here to see Lily and our mum, not you. You came here to see Lily, too, so how about you do just that and leave. For the sake of peace. How about you do that...Luka?"

"Come on, mum," Emily said softly.

Jeannie walked back into the living room with Emily, Sarah, and Mason, leaving Lily at the door to talk to Luka. At first, she didn't want to leave Lily alone in case Luka tried to get into her head again. She had willingly called Luka herself, so she must have something to say to him. Whatever it was, Jeannie decided not to interfere. Luka wouldn't hurt her, and Lily could handle herself.

---

It was close to 9 p.m. that evening when Emily, Sarah, and Mason decided to return to their hotel. They had spent their first night there at the house, but they still needed a change of clothes and a good night's rest after their travel, so Jeannie let them go. If it was up to her, she would have preferred that they spend the entire three days with her, in her home. However, when Mason called the trip a vacation, Jeannie figured she'd let them enjoy some time to themselves.

After Lily had finished talking to Luka, she had retreated to her bedroom and called it a night. Jeannie really wanted to ask Lily what she'd discussed with her father, but she managed to restrain herself. She dug up a smile for Lily and said goodnight to her before proceeding into the kitchen to clean up for the night.

As Jeannie wiped the counter, a loud knock on the door startled her. Unable to guess who it was, and concerned that the noise would wake Lily, Jeannie ran over and quickly opened the door. Without any invitation, the lady strutted into the room with her arms crossed.

"Uh, come in," Jeannie said sarcastically, shutting the door behind her. "What do you want, Isabel?"

If Jeannie was completely honest with herself, she had to admit that Isabel was a beautiful woman. She subtly assessed her from head to toe and admired how nicely the fitted, short peach gown sat on Isabel's slender body. Jeannie instinctively tightened the robe around her waist and crossed her arms.

"What do you want, Isabel?" Jeannie repeated. "It's rude to barge into a person's house this late at night. I didn't even ask you to come in."

"I'll be quick," Isabel said, playing with her ponytail. "Leave Aaron alone, Jeannie."

"Of course," Jeannie mumbled.

It was easy to predict why Isabel had come all the way to her house. They had nothing else to talk about, nothing in common. Only Aaron. Jeannie had seen this confrontation coming from the very first day she met Isabel, and she was rude to her.

"And if I say no?" Jeannie asked, tilting her head up. "What are you going to do about it? What can you do, Isabel?"

"Nothing," Isabel answered and began to pace. "But I'm not here out of jealousy, Jeannie. Or spite. I'm not here to threaten you, either."

Jeannie lifted her eyebrows. "Oh, really?"

"I am only concerned for Aaron," Isabel revealed. "Unlike you, who is only thinking about herself and how to milk Aaron of his money."

"What?" Jeannie asked, taking a step forward. "You better watch what you say, Isabel. You're in my house. You're trespassing. Did you come here to insult me?"

"Far from it," she answered. "I just came here to tell you the truth."

"Which is?"

"That you are no good for Aaron," Isabel revealed. "Did Aaron tell you about our relationship? Did he tell you how long we dated, and how we were supposed to get married?"

"From what I heard, you were forcing the marriage on him," Jeannie retorted. "Or did I hear incorrectly?"

Isabel scoffed. "I can admit that I wanted to hurry things up. But that's because I know Aaron, and I know what he wants. It was awful timing on my part that cost us our relationship, but it doesn't change the fact that you cannot give Aaron what he truly desires."

Jeannie sighed and smiled. "And what might that be, Isabel?"

"A child."

Isabel's statement hit Jeannie deep inside. Her smile waned, and she dropped her hands to the side. She had not seen it coming. Perhaps if she had, she wouldn't have been too frozen to say a word in response.

"What are you, fifty?" Isabel continued. "You cannot give Aaron a child of his own. Even if you still could, it would be very difficult and just sad. His own blood. Aaron is alone. Who is going to carry on his name? Who will inherit all his wealth? Unless that's why you're dating him, because you want it all to yourself. What Aaron wants most in this world is a child, Jeannie. One to call his own. If you were close to him like you imagine you are, you'd know this. He told me when we were dating. He wouldn't stop talking about the idea of carrying a beautiful baby that he'd do the honor of naming. That's the reason I was so keen on marrying him. You obviously cannot give him that, so why waste his time? Why waste *our* time?"

Jeannie wasn't even trying to respond to Isabel. She stood there digesting her words and wondering why she never thought about that. Why she never asked Aaron about it. Aaron didn't have a child. All he had for family was his brother who lived on the West Coast with his family. He rarely saw them. Was Jeannie truly standing in the way of Aaron's happiness?

"If you love Aaron like you claim, you will do what's best for him," Isabel continued. "I did that by letting him go the last time, but I will not sit back and watch him settle when he could have so much more. If you cannot give him what he wants, then move out of his way."

With that, Isabel stormed out of the room and slammed the door behind her. Unable to fully understand what had just happened, Jeannie remained where she stood and scanned the room. She couldn't understand why Aaron had kept this from her. For the first time since Jeannie met Isabel, she had to admit that the lady was right. Perhaps she was in the way and she needed to move.

"Mum," Lily said, walking into the living room. "What was that? I heard a lady talking a moment ago."

Jeannie forced a smile and sniffed hard, fighting back the tears threatening to fall. "It was nothing, honey. Go back to bed."

# Chapter Thirteen

*Two days later...*

The freshly brewed morning coffee that Jeannie loved to enjoy first thing in the morning suddenly had no refreshing taste to it. It was bland, almost like the numb feeling she felt on the inside. Even when she lay in bed, unable to sleep for the bulk of the night, Jeannie felt numb, too. Her mind was riddled with thoughts, and it was almost impossible to make out a coherent sentence.

Jeannie sipped from her cup of coffee and sat at the kitchen counter. She didn't want any more children. That much was certain. She had spent the past two days thinking about it. In fact, she was going through menopause, so having another child wasn't much of an option for her.

But it was an option for Aaron, and it made sense. Aaron had no child of his own, so it wasn't a far fetch to expect him to want one. Jeannie had seen how Aaron spoke to and treated Mason. It was easy to tell that he wanted a child of his own. How could she have been so blind to this?

Coming up with a solution that benefitted both of them was next to impossible. At the end of the day, one of them was going to get hurt. If Jeannie decided to be selfish and ignore the fact that she was aware of Aaron's desire for a child, then Aaron would be forced to settle. If she decided to end the relationship so Aaron could be with someone who could give him what he truly wanted, then Jeannie was going to get hurt.

"There's no way to win," Jeannie mumbled and let out a heavy sigh.

"What are you trying to win?"

Jeannie gasped and turned around at the sound of Lily's voice. "Lily," she breathed. "You startled me."

"What are you thinking about, mum?" Lily asked, standing behind Jeannie. "You've been like this ever since Emily, Mason, and Sarah arrived. Is there something else you're not telling me?"

"This has nothing to do with your siblings, I promise," Jeannie answered. "It's nothing."

"Oh, then it has something to do with Aaron, the man that comes here to see you every day. He hasn't been here in two days, and I see you ignoring his calls. Did you both fight?"

Jeannie opened her mouth to speak, but words refused to form. Apparently, Lily had been watching her. Jeannie herself didn't even realize that she had been ignoring Aaron's calls until that morning when she texted him, claiming that she was too busy with Lily to talk.

Frankly, Jeannie couldn't explain why she immediately started to avoid Aaron. From the very minute Isabel left her home two days ago, Jeannie couldn't bring herself to talk to Aaron. The thought of being an obstacle in his life, when all he had been to her was a blessing, made Jeannie uncomfortable. What had she ever done for him in the first place other than take?

"You both fought, didn't you?" Lily asked, squinting her eyes. "That's why you're not answering his calls, and that's why he hasn't come around since."

"We didn't fight," Jeannie said.

Lily raised her eyebrows. "Really?"

"Really," Jeannie answered. "Now, why are you dressed up? You can't go out yet."

"Who says?" Lily questioned. "I'm fine. I'm going to Emily's hotel to spend the day with them. Emily said they'll pick me up. They will soon be here."

Jeannie shook her head. "Lily, your arm is in a cast, and you're still limping. I think you should wait until after the final checkup at the hospital before we decide that you can—"

"Mum, come on," Lily groaned. "I'm sick of sitting inside all day long."

"You weren't sick of it before your siblings came," Jeannie responded. "You were perfectly fine with burying yourself under the covers up until your siblings arrived. Now I'm asking you to do the same thing, and you start whining."

"This is what you wanted, isn't it?" Lily asked. "Are you sure you want me to go back under the covers? 'Cos I'll do it."

Jeannie sighed and massaged her forehead with her fingers. "Fine. I was only looking out for you, that's all. If you want to go, then no one is stopping you. Have you taken your medication?"

"Yes," Lily answered, growing impatient.

"Rate the pain you're feeling now, on a scale of one to ten."

"Like a four."

Jeannie tilted her head to the side. "Are you sure?"

"Mum!" Lily protested. "I'm going now."

"I thought you said Emily was coming to pick you up."

"I'll wait outside. She should be here any minute now," Lily said. "Are you sure you're alright? Rate the pain you're feeling now, on a scale of one to ten."

Jeannie chuckled and shook her head. "Go. Make sure you're back early."

"Early?" Lily asked. "I was thinking of spending the night at the hotel."

Jeannie rose to her feet. "What? Lily!"

"Come on, mum. They are leaving tomorrow," Lily explained. "Who knows the next time I'll see them? Besides, Sarah hasn't given me the bags she bought for me, Emily promised me some cash, and Mason promised to introduce me to some of his friends. I need to hold them to their promises before they leave. Plus, the hotel is nice. I could go for a late-night swim and have all I can eat."

"You can't swim, you have a cast."

"Who says?" Lily answered and shrugged her shoulders. "The point is, I might spend the night."

Jeannie sighed again. There was no use arguing. In fact, she had to be thankful for the fact that Lily was getting along with her siblings despite their many differences. Although Jeannie knew there was something in it for Lily, she didn't mind so long as they weren't bickering like they usually did.

"Fine. Did you—"

"Yes, my pills are with me," Lily said, strolling to the door. "I'm not a child, mum. I can take care of myself. Plus, I'm used to pain. Even if I don't stuff my stomach with pain medication, I'll survive. Just...stop sulking and fix whatever it is that's wrong with you, because it's obvious."

Lily's statement broke Jeannie's heart. She hated that her daughter knew pain so well. Out of all her children, Lily had suffered the most, and yet she was the most stubborn. One would think that her many mistakes would teach her some lessons, but no. Lily always refused to learn from them. She was stubborn. Like Luka.

"Bye, mum," Lily said. "Don't wait up. Seriously."

Jeannie watched her leave before crashing on the couch. She thought of Aaron and figured that it was stupid to be ignoring him. How was she going to explain herself if he noticed? Lucky for her, Aaron was busy at work, so it was easy to blame him for their lack of communication in the past two days. However, Jeannie decided not to go her usual route of pushing things away this time and talk to Aaron about it. There was still a possibility that Isabel was lying. Thinking about it, the woman would do anything to get back into Aaron's life.

Just as Jeannie decided to pick up her phone, she heard a knock on the door. Before she could reach it, the door slowly opened, and Jeannie held her breath when she saw Aaron standing there.

"Speak of the devil," Jeannie gasped.

"Oh, so I take it you were just talking about me?" Aaron asked, taking slow steps into the room.

"Well, not talking. I was just thinking about you."

"You were?" Aaron asked. "I find that hard to believe."

A smile formed on Jeannie's face as she assessed Aaron from head to toe. It was baffling how gorgeous he looked dressed in only sweatpants and a fitted black t-shirt. For a moment, she completely forgot what they were talking about, and she took her time to admire Aaron's physique. Perhaps, if she put some effort into their morning exercises, she'd look as nice as him, too.

"Jeannie?" Aaron called her. He was standing in front of her now, with his head slightly tilted to the side as he studied her face.

"You look nice," was all Jeannie said, smiling sheepishly. Somehow, everything she had been worrying about in the past two days suddenly dissipated, and all she could see was the fine man she had come to love.

"Jeannie, you have been ignoring me for the past two days," Aaron revealed. "What's up with that?"

"Ignoring you?" Jeannie blurted. It was exactly what she

had been doing, but Aaron didn't need to confirm it. "How is that even possible?"

Aaron squinted his eyes. "Are you gaslighting me?"

"What?" Jeannie laughed awkwardly and walked over to the couch. "I don't need to. I haven't been ignoring you."

Aaron followed her and sat, too. "Jeannie. You're doing it again."

"I'm not doing anything," Jeannie said defensively. "I wasn't ignoring you. I was just a bit busy. I texted you many times."

"But you never called or answered any of my calls. Jeannie, you hate text messages, you prefer calls. You've made that clear many times. Suddenly, you don't take my calls for two days, and you start texting. What do you expect me to think?"

"Nothing. I don't want you to think of anything," Jeannie said. "You were busy. You were working, and I didn't want to disturb you. I remember you said these were important clients, and you weren't even prepared for the presentation. I didn't want to distract you."

"Okay, I'm certain that you're gaslighting me. Admit it, or I will go home," Aaron stated and crossed his arms.

Jeannie reached for his lap and squeezed it softly. "Don't be like this, Aaron."

"Admit it," Aaron said again. "I know you, Jeannie. You're forgetting that. You've done something like this before. More than once. Tell me what it is, or I'm going home."

Jeannie lowered her head. Sometimes she wondered how Aaron was able to tell things that Jeannie convinced herself she was hiding so well. Still, she had to admit that it was her fault. She was terrible at making decisions, and ignoring Aaron merely because of something his ex-lover said was a bad decision on her part.

"I'll tell you," Jeannie said after taking in a deep breath. "Isabel came to see me two days ago."

Aaron sat up on the couch. "Isabel?"

Jeannie nodded. "Yes. She said that I was standing in your way. She said a lot of things actually, a few of which hurt my feelings, but the point of her visit was to tell me that you wanted children, and since I couldn't give you any, I was being selfish by continuing this relationship."

"She had no right," Aaron said, almost in a whisper. "Why didn't you call me, Jeannie? Isabel is my problem. I would have told her off. Especially if she hurt your feelings."

Jeannie swallowed. "But did she lie?"

"What?"

"Did she lie, Aaron?" Jeannie reiterated. "You want children, don't you?"

Aaron reached for her hand and took it into his. "Jeannie—"

"Say it. Be honest with me, please. For the past two days, I've been feeling like a terrible person at the mere thought that you badly want something I cannot give you. Talk to me. I'm starting to feel like this relationship has been one-sided all this while. You know everything about me. You know my children, you know the things I love, you have helped me countless times, heck, you can even read my mind. But there's not much that I know about you. Talk to me, Aaron."

"Okay," Aaron said softly and clicked his tongue. "Isabel wasn't wrong. I will admit it. Having children has been a wish of mine for decades now. But that doesn't matter to me anymore. I just want to be with you."

"Oh, heavens," Jeannie whispered with a quaking voice. "You do want children of your own."

"Jeannie, it doesn't matter to me anymore," Aaron repeated. "If it means that I get to be with you like this, then I'm content. We're both happy. Isn't that what matters?"

"Aaron, that doesn't make it any better," Jeannie said and

sprung to her feet. "I was right to be worried about this. What kind of person would I be if I—"

Aaron stood up, too. "Jeannie, you're not listening to me," he said, trying to take her hand.

"No, you're the one not listening, Aaron. I cannot let you make that sacrifice for me. You must resent me."

"Resent you?" Aaron scoffed. "That is absurd, Jeannie. Don't make this bigger than it really is. Just listen to me. Listen to what I have to say."

"You don't resent me now, but you will eventually."

"No one is resenting anybody. Jeannie, stop. Just...hit the pause button, relax, and sit down. Let's have a conversation about this. You asked me to talk to you, but you're not listening."

In that moment, Jeannie's heart and her brain were not on the same page at all. On one hand, she wanted to sit down on that couch and allow Aaron to convince her that it wasn't a big deal, but on the other hand, this man had done too much for her for Jeannie to remain selfish. Making a decision for Aaron's sake might hurt now, but Jeannie needed to convince herself that the pain would pass in time. Knowing that she'd done the right thing would have to be enough to heal her heart. It had to be.

"Aaron, I'm sorry," Jeannie said on the verge of tears.

"No. Jeannie do not do this. You might think ending this relationship makes you the bigger person, but it really doesn't."

"I can't continue this relationship any longer," she continued. "It's not mutually beneficial, and I cannot live with that. You remember, I'm trying to put myself first this time around, right? Well, my mind wouldn't be at ease if we were to continue seeing each other. It's best to end things now. I wish you well."

"I will pretend I did not hear that," Aaron said. "Now sit and let us talk like mature adults."

"Please shut the door on your way out."

With that, Jeannie ran into her room and locked herself inside. She paused, trying to understand the emotion she was feeling in that moment, but it felt like nothing. It seemed as though her brain hadn't registered it. Jeannie expected that her head would be buried into the pillow as she wailed, but for some weird reason, she was numb. Unsure of what to feel.

"It's for the best, Jeannie," she whispered. "You know it is."

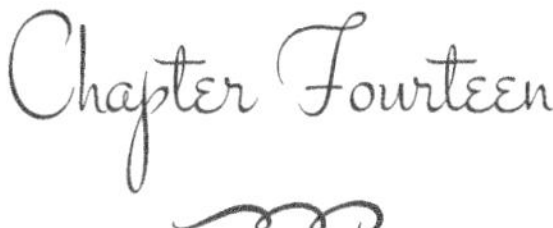

# Chapter Fourteen

"Oh, Cathy, it's horrible," Jeannie said into the phone with a muffled voice.

Her head was buried into her pillow, and Jeannie was pretty sure Cathy couldn't hear her. But she needed someone to console her and tell her that everything was going to eventually turn out fine. Jeannie was sure her heart was shredding. Her heart had been broken many times, for many different reasons, but this felt different. It was a new feeling. A scary one.

"I understand the pain, my darling," Cathy told her. "But shouldn't you be able to handle heartbreak better? I mean, you had your heart broken on countless occasions by the same man. I'd expect that you have learned from it and grown a tough skin."

"It's different," Jeannie groaned and rolled over to her stomach. "It's not the same feeling. I've never done something like this before, Cathy. I must have hurt Aaron in the process, too."

"Has he reached out since that day?"

"Yes," Jeannie sniffed. "He keeps calling, but I can't bring myself to answer the phone because I know what he's going to say. He's going to tell me not to worry about it, that it doesn't matter, when I know for a fact that it does. It matters, Cathy."

"I know, honey," Cathy cooed.

"It's even worse because I recall how I felt when I held Emily in my arms for the first time. That feeling, Cathy, of creating your own human…I really want Aaron to experience it."

"Because you love him."

"Exactly, because I love him," Jeannie continued to sob. "It would be unfair of me to stand in the way when we clearly don't want the same things, right?"

"Right."

"I mean, it's understandable that I don't want Aaron to sacrifice something so big just to be with me, right?"

"Right."

"So, I did the right thing…right?"

"Well…"

"Cathy!"

"I don't know," Cathy said through the phone. "You made a wise decision, yes, but was it the right one? I'm not so sure. Aaron is a grown adult, too, Jeannie. In the end, the decision is up to him. Not you. Or don't you want to be with him anymore?"

"Oh, you know I want that more than anything. I just don't want to be selfish."

"What happened to putting you first from now on? Or have you quickly forgotten the promise you made to yourself when you finally decided to get a restraining order against Luka?"

"Well, I was putting myself first when I called it quits with Aaron. I mean, I would be burdened by it for the rest of my life."

"You're just saying that when the truth is that all you were thinking about was Aaron. You think by doing this, you're gifting him his freedom to be with someone who can grant him his wish."

"That's one way to put it," Jeannie said. "I can't stop thinking that it's the right thing to do, Cathy. Even though it feels so wrong. I'm pretty sure if you were me, you'd be confused as to what to do, too."

"You've got that right," Cathy answered. "But like you said, you did what you thought was best. I cannot force you into making any decisions, but I really don't know what to say to make you feel any better, Jeannie. Get some rest, alright? I'm sure things will turn out fine eventually."

"Thank you, Cathy," Jeannie said with a sigh.

"Did Emily and her siblings get back safe?"

"Yes," Jeannie answered. "They called this morning. I'm sorry they couldn't stay to say hello to you, Cathy. It was a short visit."

"Oh, I understand. They are busy people. I'm surprised they could spare a few days to come here. I'll see them some other time when they visit again."

"They will. Emily said they'll visit soon once they sort out their schedules. They only came to see how Lily was doing and to get her out of bed."

"Well, they succeeded. Hopefully, the next time they come they'll stay a while."

"Hopefully," Jeannie mumbled.

"I'll call you later when I get off from work. If you need anything, don't hesitate to call me."

Once the call ended, Jeannie placed the phone on her chest and stared at the ceiling. She could admit that she was a mess. Jeannie was in tatters. If she had known that ending the relationship with Aaron was going to leave her in such a state, then perhaps she would not have done it in the first place. She had not expected to be affected like this.

"Mum?" Jeannie heard Lily say from behind her bedroom door. "Are you awake?"

Jeannie immediately sat up on the bed and wiped the tears from her cheeks. She didn't want Lily to sense that something was wrong, or else Lily would worry. There was already a lot that Lily was dealing with. Jeannie hated to add to her burden.

"Come in, Lily," she answered and cleared her throat.

Lily walked into the room holding a bouquet of flowers. They exchanged looks quietly, waiting for the other to say something.

"You...bought me flowers?" Jeannie eventually asked. "Why?"

"Not me," Lily replied. "Your man friend."

Jeannie squinted her eyes. "My man friend"—she gasped and instantly rose to her feet—"Tell him I'm not here. Tell him I went to the shop."

"He says he's just coming from the shop," Lily answered and placed the bouquet on the bed. "Have you been crying?"

"Crying? Of course not. It's just my allergies. Now, tell Aaron I'm not home."

"He knows you're home because I already told him you are," she responded.

"Why would you say that?"

"I don't know, because it's the truth. Are you saying I should have lied? What is going on with you, mum? You've been acting weird the last few days. You don't come into my room a hundred times in a day anymore. In fact, I'm the one that must come look for you now. I would have said you're starting to miss Emily, Mason, and Sarah, but we both know that's not the case. So, I am led to believe that your boyfriend is the issue. Did he do something to you?"

"Don't be absurd, Lily," Jeannie said. "Aaron's a gentleman."

"Well, gentlemen don't make you cry."

"I wasn't crying," Jeannie lied. "Now, go and tell Aaron that I'm not home. Just do something to make him leave. I don't want him to see me."

"Well, I'm pretty sure he has heard us talking by now since he's in the living room."

"Lily, do something," Jeannie whispered.

Lily brought one hand to her hip. "Are you the one breaking his heart? Is that what this is? What did you do to him?"

"Lily, I'm not having this conversation with you," Jeannie continued to whisper. "Now, do something to make him leave."

"Something like what?" Lily whispered back. "He will know I'm lying. He doesn't look stupid, mum."

"He's not. But if you ask him to leave nicely, he will. Now go."

Once Lily was gone, Jeannie scurried over to the door and placed her ear on it. She waited for a minute, and once she heard the front door shut, Jeannie dropped her head and trudged back to the bed with the flowers hugged to her chest.

"What are you doing, Jeannie Miller?" she mumbled.

---

Soon, the day became night. Jeannie hadn't moved from the bed. She hugged the flowers to her chest and just stared into space, thinking about different scenarios that only broke her heart even more. She could now understand how Lily could lie in bed all day, hidden under the covers, and not feel the need to go out for fresh air like Jeannie always clamored for. It didn't even feel like twelve hours had passed.

The rumble in her stomach was getting louder. Jeannie was starving, but she lacked the will to stand up and do something about it. She was comfortable in that position, and she feared that if she moved around, she'd find another reason to cry again.

It hadn't even been that long since she'd ended the relationship with Aaron, yet Jeannie missed him so much. If only there was a way around the situation. If only she didn't have to sacrifice her happiness to do one good thing for Aaron. Why wasn't anything going her way?

"Mum?" Lily said.

Jeannie hadn't realized that Lily had walked into the room. She groaned as she turned around and stared at Lily.

"Yes, Lily?" she said with a croaked voice.

Lily set the tray in her hand down and sat by Jeannie on the bed. "I don't understand what's going on with you, and I'm starting to worry. It's a new feeling. Usually, you're the one worrying about me, but now, I can't even sleep because you're like this. Did someone die?"

"No," Jeannie answered. She pulled herself up from the bed and leaned on the frame. "No, Lily. Thinking about it, I'm the one choosing to punish myself. It's just...there is so much happening so fast that it's hard to keep track. I'm sorry if it seems like I'm neglecting you. I'm just not in the right frame of mind to do anything right now."

"I can see that," Lily said. "You haven't been to the shop in three days, you're not eating, you're crying—"

"I'm not—"

"Stop denying it, mum," Lily said, shaking her head. "Just, don't. I'm not a child like you might believe. I have had my own fair share of heartbreak, and I have broken some hearts, too. Believe it or not, I know heartbreak when I see it. So, tell me. What did Aaron do?"

"Nothing," Jeannie answered, pulling the tray of soup toward her.

"Mum—"

"He didn't do anything, Lily," Jeannie explained. 'That's why it hurts so much."

Lily adjusted on the bed and faced Jeannie. "So, *you* did something."

"No. It's what I cannot do for him that has caused this mess," Jeannie revealed.

"I'm not following, mum. Don't speak in riddles. Tell me what happened," Lily asked. "Like it or not, I am an expert in this field. I know better than you when it comes to love."

Jeannie rolled her eyes and smiled weakly. "Aaron wants children. I cannot give him children. So, what's the use of being together if I cannot grant his one wish?"

"Oh…"

They sat in silence as Jeannie sipped her soup quietly. Talking about it wasn't a good idea. The mere thought that she and Aaron were over always summoned the waterworks, and talking about it made the entire situation sound pitiful.

"What did he say about it? When you spoke to him. You spoke to him about it, right?"

"What's there to say, Lily?" Jeannie asked, feeling a lump in her throat. "I know that Aaron really cares about me. He does, and in the past, he has sacrificed so much for me. But what have I ever done for him in return? Nothing. He paid for your hospital bill, Lily. If it wasn't for him, I wouldn't have that bakery and those loyal employees. Aaron has done so much to help me."

Lily's forehead furrowed. "And your solution was to break his heart?"

"He'll heal," she answered. "We'll both heal. But I know that when all this blows over, Aaron will thank me. I'm doing this for him."

"Did he ask you to do it for him?"

"He doesn't need to ask. I'm not stupid, Lily. Neither am I

inconsiderate. Let's say we continued the relationship and eventually we got married. Because if I'm being totally honest, that's what I want, Lily. I want to marry Aaron. I want to spend the rest of my life with him. But I'm not young anymore. I cannot give him any more children. Aaron has no one. His only relative is his brother who lives far from here. It would be nice if he had a child of his own. Someone to carry on his last name. I cannot give him this. Would it not be selfish to hold on to him?"

"Did you talk to him at least?" Lily asked. "Did he tell you that he wants children?"

"Yes," Jeannie answered. "He said it himself."

"Then why is he still bringing you flowers and asking that you take his calls?" Lily asked. "I mean, it doesn't add up, if you ask me."

"Lily, you don't understand. Sometimes...when you love someone, the best thing to do for them is to let them go."

Lily scoffed. "You read that in a book, didn't you?"

Jeannie shrugged her shoulders. "I'm not sure I said it right, but you get my point."

Lily paused for a minute. "I do. I understand your perspective, but you cannot make decisions for other people, mum. If he is still coming here with expensive roses, then he must not care that you cannot give him what he wants. Sometimes, it's not sacrifice. Priorities change. You might be more important now. Did you think of that?"

Jeannie swallowed. "It's not fair. It's not fair to Aaron, and I won't let him keep sacrificing and providing for me when I do very little for him. I don't want to be a burden in his life, Lily. You understand, don't you?"

"I do. I also know that you jump to conclusions a lot, mum. You think the worst of every situation and brace yourself for it. That's what you're doing now."

"You sound just like Aaron," Jeannie mumbled, fiddling with her food. "It's not always a bad thing, you know. If you have thought of every possible thing that could happen, I guarantee that nothing will surprise you."

"Sometimes surprises are good, and you're doing it wrong," Lily said. "It's not your place to make this decision."

"What's done is done, Lily," Jeannie said. "You'll see that in time, I did what's right."

Lily sighed. "Fine. If you say so. Now, eat your food before it gets cold."

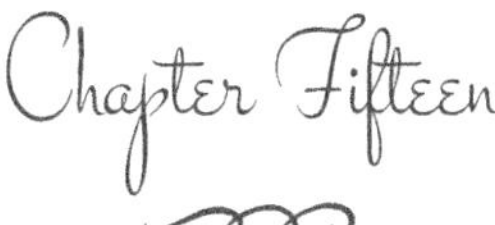

# Chapter Fifteen

The shop was filled with so much chatter, Jeannie could barely hear herself think. She had quickly forgotten how great it made her feel to see the crowd that visited her small shop every single day. It hadn't been that long since she started the business, and yet they turned a good amount of profit at the end of each day. Jeannie received a lot of compliments, too. Spending time at the shop was a much better option than sitting in her bedroom wallowing in self-pity.

"Jeannie..."

"Yes?" Jeannie replied instinctively before turning around.

"Can I speak to you for a minute?" Denise asked.

"Absolutely. Let's go into the kitchen. It's a bit noisy in here."

Jeannie strolled in front of Denise and stopped when they walked through the kitchen doors. She leaned on the counter paying close attention to Denise.

"Is there an issue, Denise?" she asked. "You can talk to me."

"Not at all," Denise answered and stuffed her hands into

her back pocket. "It's just...we have noticed something about you, and I figured I'd ask you about it. You know..."

Jeannie inhaled sharply. "Denise, I know it seems as if I don't take the bakery seriously. Especially in the last few weeks, but I promise—"

"No, no, that's not it," Denise said, waving her hands in the air. "Please. You're the owner of the bakery, Jeannie. You can do whatever you want. That's what you have us for. To do the work. Why would I question you about something like that? I'm the employee, Jeannie."

"Oh." Jeannie mellowed and smiled. "I'm sorry. You all have been doing such a great job taking care of the shop. I sincerely couldn't have asked for better employees."

"Aww, thank you," Denise beamed. "It means so much hearing you say this, Jeannie. Thank you."

"You're welcome," she said. "Now, what was it you wanted to ask me?"

"How are you, Jeannie?" Denise asked. "I mean, Lily is out of the hospital, thank God, but you still don't look well, Jeannie. Is there something else going on? Did the doctors say anything about Lily's health? You seem distant."

Jeannie dropped her shoulders and exhaled. She was wearing her broken heart on her sleeve. Was it really that obvious?

"It's not Lily, Denise," Jeannie answered. "It's me. I admit I've been distant, but it's only because I'm going through something right now. But I promise, all of that will soon be over and I will be better. Trust me."

"Do you want to talk about it?"

"I'd rather not," Jeannie said. "But I assure you, it's not a big deal. I can be a very dramatic person. I'll be alright, Denise. I promise."

"Alright. In the meantime, don't worry about the bakery at

all," Denise told her. "We have everything under control until you are ready to fully return. Plus, if you need anything, you know we are here to help you. As employees and as new friends."

Jeannie felt tears sting her eyes. "That's good to hear, Denise. I've never been able to brag about having friends, you know. I only had Cathy, all my life. But it's good to know I have people I can count on."

"Yes, you do." Denise smiled. "I think you should go home, Jeannie. You really don't look well."

"Oh, that's just because I've been crying," Jeannie explained. "I look like a mess, don't I?"

"A pretty mess," Denise joked.

"I think I'll just take your advice and head out," Jeannie said, stretching. "It's almost time to close, and I've left Lily at home for too long."

"How is Lily?" Denise asked.

"She's getting better. She says the headaches have reduced, the body pain, too. Although her leg still hurts, and we can't remove the cast for another week. Sometimes she gets dizzy or nauseous, but the doctor said it's normal. Give her a few weeks, and she'll be back to normal."

"That's good to hear," Denise said. "I wish her a speedy recovery."

"Thank you, Denise." Jeannie smiled. "I'll see you tomorrow."

"See you tomorrow, Jeannie."

Jeannie picked up her small bag and made her way out of the kitchen. She said goodbye to the workers and to some of the customers she knew before making her way home.

She really wanted to talk to Aaron. There was no doubt about it. Jeannie had been considering the option of staying friends with Aaron, even though they weren't together anymore. It wasn't impossible, but she doubted that Aaron would agree. He had been against the breakup in the first place. How could she possibly ask him to be her friend?

"I'm home, Lily," Jeannie announced as she walked into the house.

"Before you say anything…"

There was no telling if it was fear, excitement, or anxiety that had overwhelmed Jeannie in that moment, but whatever it was caused her to freeze on the spot. She stared directly at Aaron, seated in her living room with Lily. For a moment, the room went completely silent before Jeannie's bag dropped to the floor.

"Aaron," she managed to say.

"Jeannie," he answered, copying her tone. "You look like you've seen a ghost."

"I invited him over," Lily announced. "I'm sorry I didn't tell you, but I stole his number from your phone yesterday when you were in the bathroom sobbing for three hours. I couldn't take it anymore."

"I wasn't sobbing, I was taking a bath," Jeannie argued.

"Right. Just yesterday, you were in the kitchen making a sandwich for over an hour. That's not normal. You've been depressed for the past week and it's not a pretty sight to see every single day."

Jeannie glanced at Aaron and swallowed. She could feel the heat rise in her cheeks, and it was difficult trying to mask the smile on her lips.

"I called Aaron here today to talk to him about your relationship," Lily continued, "But it turns out that you, mother, jumped the gun. Like you always do."

Lily walked over to Jeannie's side and pulled her into the living room. "So, how about you sit down and talk to Aaron about your relationship. I only sat down to talk to him for thirty minutes, and I can confidently say he's my favorite person in the entire world now."

Jeannie's eyes widened. "What?" she blurted. "Where did that come from?"

"I'm serious," Lily said. "I think I like him a bit more than I like you, mum."

"Lily!" Jeannie said and smacked her on the arm.

"I'm kidding," Lily groaned. "Or maybe I'm not. You'll never know. Now, sit and listen, mum."

Lily glanced back and forth at the both of them, then exited the room. Jeannie turned and pretended to watch her as an excuse to remain silent and figure out what in the world she was going to say to Aaron.

"Jeannie," Aaron called her gently.

A tingling wave coursed through her entire body at the sound of his voice. Jeannie held her breath, bit her lower lip, and turned back around to face him.

"Hello, Aaron."

"You're cruel," he stated.

"I'm sorry," Jeannie answered. "But you know it's for the best."

"Best for who? Me? Or you?"

"You, of course. Why would I do this for me? I have nothing to benefit from us parting ways."

"Neither do I, now sit," he demanded. "And stay quiet because I think you've said enough. It's my turn to speak, don't you think?"

Jeannie exhaled loudly and sat like he had instructed. She crossed her legs and looked everywhere except at Aaron's face. Deep down, Jeannie was thrilled that she could finally talk to Aaron again, despite what she did.

"Aaron, nothing you say is going to change my mind," Jeannie said, secretly hoping he wouldn't take her statement as a cue to leave.

"Oh, really?" he asked, sitting by her side. "So, you're determined not to make this work?"

Jeannie faced him swiftly. "Of course not. I want this to work, but there is nothing we can do about it. Aaron, I don't want to keep seeing you if it makes me feel guilty."

"Guilty about what? All I ask is that you don't make decisions for me, Jeannie. It's my choice."

"You admitted that you wanted a child. Isabel said it, and you confirmed it."

"What did Isabel tell you?" Aaron asked. "Tell me what she said."

Jeannie sat back on the chair and crossed her arms. "She said you wanted a child, and when she tried to rush the wedding, you bailed."

"Did I not already tell you how our relationship ended?"

"You did, but that's not what matters right now, Aaron," Jeannie said. "I know Isabel isn't a trustworthy person, but it doesn't change the fact that there was some truth in what she said."

"There was, yes, I admit it," Aaron said. "But that changed, Jeannie."

Jeannie groaned. "Oh, don't say it changed when you met me. That just makes it worse. It means you're settling."

"Would you stop talking? Please?" Aaron asked. "Don't put words in my mouth. Let me talk to you."

Jeannie sighed and mellowed. "Sorry."

"Thank you. Now, like I was trying to explain," Aaron started, "Isabel and me. Like I told you before, we had good times together. But I didn't just walk away from the relationship. When I told Isabel I wanted children, it was because I thought there was a chance that I could have one. So, I put it out there that having a child would be nice. But immediately after I said that to her, she became obsessed with the idea. She started moving way too fast. Started making plans for a wedding, started granting interviews, making statements...it became too much. That was the reason I walked away."

"It still doesn't—"

"Jeannie."

"Sorry," she said. "I'm listening."

"I have children now," Aaron said. "I'm currently going out with this amazing woman who worries so much, it's frustrating, who is caring, who loves to cook, and who cares for her kids more than anything in this world. It might sound weird, but I consider her children to be mine now. I promise you, this is all I want in life right now. You and your children."

Jeannie took his hand. "Aaron, I don't want you to settle. I don't want that."

"I'm not settling. Things change, Jeannie. You have no control over such things. What I want now is a life with you. I thought you wanted that, too."

"Of course, I do. You know I do."

"No, I don't. I don't know, Jeannie, because you confuse me. I'm not a child, Jeannie. I am a grown man. I know what I want, and I have made that clear from the moment I met you. Did I ever waiver?"

Jeannie lowered her head.

"Jeannie, did I ever waiver?"

"No," she said quietly.

"Did I give you a reason to doubt me?"

"No."

"Did I give you a reason to believe that you weren't enough?"

"No, you didn't."

"Then where is this coming from?"

Jeannie ran her fingers through her hair and sat back. "It is what's best for you. In the end, you'll be happy. I want you to be fulfilled, Aaron."

"Who says I'm not happy?" Aaron asked. "Jeannie, in the

end, I am the only one responsible for my own happiness. If I say it's with you, then I won't stop chasing you. Except if you report me to the police for stalking. Then I'll stop."

Jeannie chuckled. "Don't make jokes, Aaron. This is serious."

"It's not really," Aaron said. "I want to be with you, Jeannie. You and no one else. Do you want to be with me?"

Jeannie paused for a moment, but it wasn't to think. She just didn't want to sound too eager. "Yes," she said clearly.

Before Aaron could reply, Jeannie leaned in and placed a gentle kiss on his lips. She meant to pull away, but Aaron held her in place by her nape and pulled her further into his embrace.

"I missed you," Jeannie whispered.

"And whose fault is that?"

Jeannie laughed and fell into his arms. "I'm sorry. I thought I was doing what was best, but I should have just listened to you."

"You have a habit of doing that, you know?" Aaron said. "I keep telling you, but you refuse to change."

"I will," Jeannie groaned. "I'm just not used to...this, yet. It shocks me to say this, but my daughter Lily is more experienced than me when it comes to this. I had no idea she stole your number from my phone. I don't even know how she unlocked it. Apparently, all the nights she snuck out of the house to party paid off."

Aaron chuckled. "I'm glad she called me."

"By the way..." Jeannie lifted her head and met his gaze. "What did Lily mean when she said you were now her favorite person in the world?"

Aaron shrugged his shoulders. "I don't know what you're talking about."

Jeannie squinted her eyes. "Aaron...what did you say to her?"

"Don't worry about it," Aaron said, pulling her into his embrace. "I'm still mad at you for letting me miss Mason when he came. If only you'd picked up the phone. I wanted to invite him and his sisters over to my place for dinner, but I had to ask you first."

"I'm sorry. They only stayed three days," Jeannie said. "Apparently, they flew all the way here just to make sure Lily was okay. I reckon they'll visit again soon. At least, that's what they said."

"They better. I'll fly them in myself," Aaron said. "I felt so bad when Lily told me they had left."

"I'm sorry," Jeannie groaned. "If you had come on the first day, you might have met them. But they spent the remaining two days at the hotel having fun with Lily."

Aaron sighed. "Oh well."

Jeannie smiled sheepishly and shut her eyes. She wouldn't have imagined that a day would come when she'd be grateful to Lily for something she did. For once, Lily had done something nice for her, and Jeannie was never going to forget it.

---

"What did you and Aaron talk about?"

Jeannie had not seen Lily smile that brightly in a while, and she found it both thrilling and unsettling. Lily was hiding something. After Aaron had left at close to midnight, she had emerged from her room giggling. Jeannie had managed to sit her down by bribing her with some snacks, but she was still holding back information from her.

"You really want to know?" Lily asked, giving Jeannie a witty, devious look. "You wanna know, mum?"

"Just tell me already," Jeannie asked. "Aaron was

convinced you didn't like him and then suddenly, he's your favorite person in the world. That doesn't just happen."

"Alright, fine," Lily said, giggling. "Aaron promised me a trip to the Bahamas once I recover. A fully funded two-week's vacation, mum. To the Bahamas!"

"What?" Jeannie blurted. "He did?"

"Oh, don't start whining that he didn't inform you," Lily said. "I told him you wouldn't mind. It's my decision anyway. Isn't it, mum?"

"Of course," Jeannie said. "It's just...surprising, that's all. You asked for a bribe, didn't you, Lily?"

"No! That's the thing. I didn't have to ask. Apparently, your boyfriend is rich, mum. Not just that, he has his way with words. He knew the things I like, which I think is because you told him, but...anyway, the point is, he has my blessing."

Jeannie slapped Lily's arm. "When will you stop being materialistic? Aaron is more than his money."

"That's for you to know," she replied. "All I care about is the fact that he is generous."

"I won't let you—"

"I won't," Lily groaned. "I'm not stupid. If I ask him for stuff, he'll go away. Plus, I don't think I need to ask. He looks like the type that just gives. And I like that about him. I like it a lot."

Jeannie shook her head. "Where did you come from?"

Lily giggled. "But, seriously speaking. He's good, mum. It takes a lot to impress me, but it only took five minutes of talking to Aaron to do just that. He means well for you, and I can see that he likes you a lot. Which surprises me because you—"

"Don't. Say it," Jeannie cautioned. "Whatever it is you wanted to say, just keep it to yourself. I know I have many flaws, but I'm working on them."

"Good. We're all works in progress," Lily said. "I'm sure Aaron has his flaws, too."

"He really doesn't. He is literally perfect."

"Right," Lily said sarcastically.

They giggled and sighed at the same time. Jeannie stared at Lily's happy face, and for a moment, she hesitated to ask her about Luka. But it seemed like the right thing to do.

"Lily," Jeannie said softly. "About your...uhm..."

"About my father?" Lily voiced. "I know you've been dying to find out what we talked about the other day, and why I called him over in the first place."

"You don't have to tell me if you don't want to," Jeannie said.

Lily lowered her head. "Can I not tell you then? It's nothing, but I just don't want to talk about my father right now. I want to heal and think about it with a clear head. He says he never intended to hurt me, and he was trying to make up for it, and for some reason, I believe him. But then again, I'm not blind to everything he put the family through. I might not have experienced it or felt his absence because I was born late, and I had you and my siblings to fill the gap, but he's still my father, mum. I don't know what to do right now, but let me think about it on my own time."

"That's fine, my love," Jeannie said. "Whenever you're ready."

## Chapter Sixteen

*Two weeks later...*

"Mum, we're out of apple pies and it's not even 12 p.m. yet? What do we do? I promised that old lady across the street that I'd keep one for her when she comes at two, but we don't have any."

Jeannie took off her gloves. "Well, why did you make her a promise if you didn't stash one away for her, Lily?"

"I forgot," Lily answered with a bewildered look on her face. "Don't tell me we're all out? There's none in the kitchen?"

"Give me one moment, let me check the back," Jeannie said and chuckled. "Of course, there's none in the kitchen. Once it's baked and ready, it goes into the glass. You know this."

Lily groaned. "Oh, what am I going to do? Should I hide in the kitchen when she comes?"

"No. You're going to go back to the counter, wait for her to arrive, apologize, and promise her that you will give her one for free tomorrow. One you will pay for from your own pocket."

"What? Mum!" Lily whined.

"Yes, Lily. Next time, when you make a promise, keep it."

Lily stomped her feet on the ground and walked back to the counter. Seeing her in an apron with a funny cap working behind the counter amused Jeannie. There had been a line of flour on Lily's cheek ever since that morning, but no one had said anything to her about it because it was funny and cute at the same time. But Jeannie knew if Lily found out she had been walking around like that all day, she was going to get mad.

Lily always said she didn't like corporate work, and she would rather do anything else. But in the past three days, she had been coming to the bakery religiously and helping with the baking and the sales. She even made friends with all the workers. It pleased Jeannie to have Lily so close to her. It had been a month since she woke up, and not once had she talked about going back to New York. Jeannie secretly prayed it stayed that way. Having Lily around warmed her heart.

Soon, it was time for their break, and Jeannie hastily made her way to the front. Aaron had made a routine of visiting her during lunch to spend some time with her before he had to head back to work, and before she had to continue baking. They would sit at an empty booth and talk about the most random things. It was always the highlight of Jeannie's day.

"Mum, your boyfriend is here," Jeannie heard Lily say as she walked into the shop.

Just as Lily had announced, Aaron walked into the shop dressed in a nice black suit and tie. But he was not alone. With him was a much younger man. Probably about Lily's age...or older, Jeannie couldn't tell. He was what Lily always referred to as a 'pretty boy' anytime they were watching TV. He had nice features. Tall, dark, fluffy hair, a chiseled jawline, and aquamarine eyes. His features were like Aaron's. Too similar.

"Woah, is that his son?" Lily asked Jeannie, standing by

her side. She still had her apron on, and the flour was still on her face.

"I'm not even sure," Jeannie mumbled.

Aaron approached Jeannie with a grin on his face and hugged her in her frozen state. "What? Why are you so surprised?"

"Who is this handsome young man?" Jeannie asked.

Aaron placed his hand on the boy's shoulder and squeezed. "Jeannie, I would like you to meet Reuben Horn."

"Horn?" Jeannie said and gasped. "Aaron, is he—you didn't tell me you had—"

"A nephew. I have a nephew, Jeannie. He's my brother's son, and he's here visiting."

"Oh," was all Jeannie said. For some reason, hearing that Reuben was Aaron's son would have been more exciting. "Hello, Reuben. It's good to meet you. I'm Jeannie, Aaron's girlfriend."

"Good afternoon, ma'am," Aaron said, shaking Jeannie's hand. "I've heard a lot about you from my uncle. You look even prettier in person."

"In person?" Jeannie smiled. "You've seen pictures of me?"

"Oh, yes. Uncle Aaron has an entire folder on his laptop with your pictures," he answered.

Aaron sucked in his teeth. "Reuben, if you say it like that, it makes it sound weird. I don't have a folder. I showed you a few pictures. That's all you should have said."

"Sorry," Reuben whispered.

"I'm not surprised," Jeannie said. "I have a folder with his pictures on my laptop, too."

"Ah, I see the spark between you two now," Reuben joked.

"Reuben, meet my daughter Lily," Jeannie introduced her. "She's a model in New York, but she's currently helping me out here in the shop."

"Good day to you, Lily," Reuben said and stretched his hand toward Lily.

Lily took her time to respond. She just stared at him with squinted eyes. "You sound like a textbook."

"Lily," Jeannie rasped. "Be nice."

"A textbook?" Reuben asked. "What does that mean?"

"Who greets like that?" Lily asked. "Good day to you? What are you doing? Sending an email? Who says that?"

Reuben dropped his hand and scoffed. "Nice apron."

Jeannie snorted and hid behind Aaron so Lily didn't see her laughing. Wearing an apron that read "I'm adorable from head to-ma-toes" ruined her sassy approach. Jeannie wondered why Lily had chosen that apron in the first place, but she said nothing about it. If Reuben said a word about the flour on Lily's cheek, Jeannie didn't want to imagine how red Lily would get.

As if he'd read her mind, Reuben reached for Lily's cheek and wiped off the flour with his thumb. "Very adorable," he said. "You even bake with your face."

"Oh, god," Jeannie whispered, fighting back the urge to laugh. "Lily's going to kill him."

"I think Reuben is a good match for her," Aaron whispered back. "He might be very well-mannered, but he has a way with words."

"Like you?"

"Exactly like me," Aaron said.

"You think you're funny," Lily told Reuben.

"I do," he answered. "Would you like to hear a joke?"

"Save it," Lily said and stormed away. He paused a few feet away and turned around, her face flushed crimson. "It was not nice to meet you."

"Aw, why?" Reuben asked. "I found you adorable."

"Shut up," Lily said and untied the apron as she continued to storm away.

"You know, Reuben," Jeannie said. "You are the first person I've seen to get Lily that embarrassed. She usually wins every argument."

"Oh, we have that in common," Reuben said.

"Reuben is studying law," Aaron explained. "He's on break now for a couple of weeks, so I invited him here to meet you and Lily. You see, Reuben likes to bake. So, when I told him that my girlfriend runs a bakery, he jumped on the idea of coming here."

"I would like to work here, if you will have me, ma'am," Reuben said. "I promise my main aim is to learn. I won't be any trouble and I am as humble as they come."

Jeannie crossed her arms. "First off, don't call me ma'am. My name is Jeannie. And second, all you had to do was ask. I would love to have you, Reuben."

"Thank you, Jeannie," Reuben said. "I am at your service."

"I'm glad," Jeannie said. "I'll show you around the bakery and introduce you to everyone."

"I'd like that."

Jeannie glanced at Aaron and smiled when he mouthed a 'thank you.' She ushered Reuben further into the shop, and they made their way to the kitchen. More than anything, she was excited to see how Reuben and Lily would interact with each other. Their first encounter had been very pleasing to watch.

"So, tell me, Reuben." Jeannie cleared her throat. "What's college like?"

---

Jeannie was sitting behind the counter cleaning out the trays when Reuben approached her. In the space of two days, the boy had managed to grow on her. Jeannie had come to like him, so much that she would seek him out and sit him down for a chat. He had a lot to say, and when he spoke, he sounded so much like Aaron, it pleased Jeannie.

"Jeannie, I think my wrists are about to fall off at this point," Reuben said and sat on the stool. "Kneading isn't easy work."

"That's why we have a machine that kneads, Reuben." Jeannie chuckled. "I only told you to mix the ingredients, but you don't listen."

"I'm not complaining," he said. "I like to knead. But damn, it's a lot of work."

Jeannie glanced at Reuben's apron and stifled a smile. "You know that apron belongs to Lily, right? I mean, it's not technically hers, but it's the one she likes to wear when she comes around."

"Oh," Reuben said, assessing it. "I figured I'd wear it because it fits me better. Plus, if you think about it, I think I'm more adorable than Lily, so I should have the apron."

"Are you hitting on my mum?"

Jeannie lifted her head and found Lily standing behind Reuben. She had no idea where she came from, but she was glad she did. Now, all Jeannie had to do was sit back and watch Reuben and Lily bicker.

"Hitting on her?" Reuben asked, turning around. "You're really asking me if I'm hitting on my uncle's girlfriend?"

Lily shrugged her shoulders. "There's nothing new under the sun. Who knows? You might have a thing for older women."

"You're wrong, I have a thing for adorable ladies," Reuben answered.

Lily rolled her tongue in her mouth. "You're not going to drop that, are you?"

"Nope."

"You're petty."

"I know. Do you like what I'm wearing? Jeannie says it's your special apron, but I think we can share it. That's if you find me adorable, too."

"Lily thinks you're a pretty boy," Jeannie chimed in, in a bid to add fuel to the already flaming fire.

"I do not," Lily said, louder than necessary. "Why would you say that, mum?"

"What?" Reuben said. "I like to think I'm pretty."

"No. Timothee Chalamet is pretty. You're just a nerd."

"Those two things aren't mutually exclusive," Reuben said.

"What do you mean?"

"I mean, I can be a nerd and still be a pretty boy."

Lily scoffed. "Name one, pretty nerd."

"Me. Reuben Horn. Name another," he said.

Lily opened her mouth to speak but she paused instead. She turned to Jeannie and then back to Reuben. "Shut up," was all she said.

"Oh, goodness gracious, will you two stop bickering all the time?" Jeannie asked. "Lily, you fight with every single person that comes your way. Even your siblings. Try and get along with Reuben. It was cute at first, and I thought this might turn out to be like an enemy-to-lovers book I read, but you both are dragging the plot. Find a common ground already. Reuben, what's your favorite activity?"

"Hiking," he answered.

"Gross," Lily said.

Reuben arched his eyebrows. "Why is that gross?"

"Why would you like to hike? It's pointless and stressful."

"It's not pointless. I think it's refreshing. A way to recharge your energy."

"How do you recharge your energy when you're using it all up by hiking?"

Reuben inhaled sharply. "Fair point. What's your favorite activity?"

"I don't think I have one," Lily said.

"What's your favorite...anything?" Reuben asked. "Food, movie, song..."

"There's not a lot of things I like," Lily stated.

Reuben examined her from head to toe. "You like long sleeves. I've been here three days and that's all you wear, even when it's hot. I think that's suspicious because you also have a habit of pulling your sleeves so far down that they cover your hands."

Jeannie clumsily dropped the tray and the sound grabbed Reuben's attention. He turned to her, and instantly Jeannie could tell he'd read her facial expression. He turned to look at Lily, then he looked back at Jeannie. The sudden silence must have confirmed it for him. Reuben rose to his feet and faced Lily.

"Don't," Lily said, moving away. "It's not..."

"I'm sorry," Reuben said quietly.

"For what? Don't apologize."

"I should have watched my words. I didn't think..."

"It's alright, Reuben," Jeannie told him. "Lily is way past that. She's better now. Right, Lily?"

Lily forced a smile. "Of course. It's nothing, Reuben. Really."

Even though they were trying to make him feel better, Reuben still looked sorry. It was the first time Jeannie had seen him like this. He must have been so scared that he touched a sensitive subject. Reuben had put two and two together so easily. Lily always hid the marks on her wrists with her long sleeves. So far, no one had questioned her about it.

"I was sixteen...I think," Lily said. "It wasn't a big deal. Frankly, I don't know why I did it. The wound wasn't deep enough to kill me, but...it left a scar. I'm not hiding it from the world, I'm hiding the marks from myself. I don't care if people see it, I just don't want to see it."

"Because you don't want to be reminded of it?"

"Because seeing it makes me hate myself," Lily said. "Like I said, I still don't know why I did it. I've always been a mess since I was little. Been depressed since I was twelve. Things are better now, that's why I don't like to think of that time."

Reuben tapped her on the arm. "You might be a mess, but at least you're an adorable one."

Lily giggled, the loudest Jeannie had heard her laugh in a long time. "Shut up, Reuben. And take off my apron."

Reuben nodded. "Can I give you a hug? Please? It's not for you, I just feel like a terrible person right now for making you bring it up."

Lily glanced at Jeannie. "Sure," she said to Reuben. "But you only get five seconds."

Reuben placed his arms around Lily's shoulders and patted her back. Knowing that somehow Lily had managed to make a new friend pleased Jeannie. She was terrible at it. The kind of company Lily used to keep worried Jeannie. Lily never had friends that thought it was necessary to introduce themselves to Jeannie. They would come around the house, blasting their loud music and screaming Lily's name. For the first time, Jeannie was glad to see Lily being friendly with a good person.

"What is this I see?"

Aaron's voice came as a shock to all of them. He stood by the entrance, studying Lily and Reuben.

"You see, I knew this was going to happen," he continued. "I just knew it."

"It's not what it looks like, uncle," Reuben said, breaking the hug.

"Well, whatever it is, I like it," he said.

"Aaron, soon I'll hold you to the promise you made me," Lily said, approaching Aaron. "You haven't forgotten, right?"

Aaron stroked her hair and shook his head. "Whenever you're ready, just say the word. I'll have someone make all the arrangements."

"Yes," Lily whispered, jumping excitedly. "Thank you."

"You're welcome," he said. "In the meantime, how about a double date? I have this nice restaurant I'm planning on taking Jeannie to tomorrow night. Would you both like to come? We could make it a thing."

"Of course," Lily said without hesitation. "I can't recall the last time I've been to a nice restaurant."

"Good," Aaron said. "Reuben?"

Reuben walked up to Lily. "Lily, would you be my date tomorrow?"

Lily tilted her head to the side. "Hasn't that already been established?"

"Lily!" Jeannie called from behind the counter. "Be nice."

"Why can't I be Aaron's date?" she joked.

"Because I'm your mother's date," Aaron answered. "Now, don't leave Reuben hanging. He is trying to be a gentleman."

"I am," Reuben said. "Now say yes, or I will burn your apron to ashes."

Lily giggled. "Fine. Wear something nice. Aaron says it's a fancy restaurant."

"We should decide on a color to wear," Reuben said. "Come on. Let's go to the kitchen. You can help me knead the dough."

Lily followed behind him. "Oh, hell no. My arm will break."

"That's because you have twigs for arms. I oughta stuff you with three cheeseburgers every day."

"Be my guest. I love cheeseburgers."

"Me too."

Jeannie couldn't stop watching them. They reminded her of a time when she had thought she was the happiest person in the world. A time when Luka had not yet decided to ruin her life. And it was all thanks to Aaron. Her boyfriend.

Jeannie turned to Aaron and stretched both hands toward him with a wide grin on her face. "Come here," she beamed.

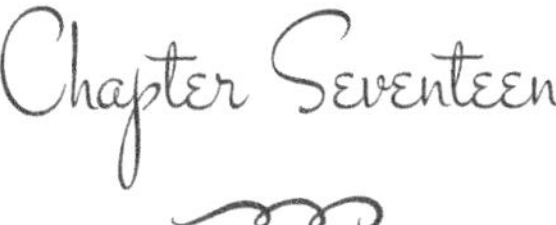

# Chapter Seventeen

"A date? Lily's going on a date? With a decent man? Like an actual person?"

When Jeannie had informed her three other children that Lily not only got along with a boy but agreed to a date, they didn't want to believe it. Back in New York, Lily had a thing for breaking hearts. She changed boyfriends like clothes and made a play to collect things from them before she even agreed to a date.

"Stop making it seem like a big deal and help me choose something to wear," Lily said, pacing Jeannie's room.

"She has been restless since this afternoon," Jeannie said. "The date's in about an hour, and she still hasn't decided on what to wear. I've told her that the three dresses she bought are pretty, but she keeps saying I'm not being honest."

"She's right," Sarah said. "Anything Lily puts on will be beautiful in your eyes, but you know me, I won't lie to her. Lily, let me see the first dress."

Lily scurried over to the bed and picked up a blue, fitted gown with sparkles on it. She held it against her body and stood in front of the screen. "Okay, listen. It has a slit on the left leg. It's high. The lace on the shoulders blends so well with my skin that you can hardly see it."

"It's horrible," Emily said.

"Is it for prom?" Mason asked.

"Seriously, why would you buy this?"

"Be nice," Jeannie cautioned. "Jeez. I think the dress is beautiful. Blue is Lily's color."

"No, black is," Sarah said.

"I got a black dress!" Lily announced excitedly. She ran over to the bed again and soon returned with a dress. "Now this one is adorned with pearls around the bust area alone. It's short in the front and long at the back. The sleeves are long, and it's a V-neck cut."

"It'll do," Sarah said.

"I don't know," Mason chimed in. "It might show some cleavage."

"What's wrong with some cleavage?" Emily asked.

"Everything," he answered.

"It won't," Sarah assured him. "Lily barely has anything on her chest to show. She'll be fine."

"You know what? I'm in a good mood, so I will ignore your remarks, Sarah," Lily said. "But thank you for your input. Now, my hair. Up or down?"

"Up," the three of them said simultaneously.

"With pearl earrings," Sarah added. "Ask mum for a pair. If you can, wear a red lipstick."

"Thank you so much, Sarah," Lily said and scurried out of the room with her gown to get dressed.

"It's been a while since I've seen her this excited about something," Jeannie told them. "I think she's trying to prove to Reuben that she's hot, not adorable."

"Who is this Reuben?" Emily asked.

"Oh, he's Aaron's nephew who came to Chickadee Cove for his break," Mason explained. "He's twenty-two years old, studying law, and he currently works at mum's bakery to pass time. Aaron says he's a nice kid."

"Am I dating Aaron or are you, Mason Miller?" Jeannie asked him. "I think you talk to him more than you talk to me."

"That's probably true," Mason answered. "I wish I had stayed a bit longer in Chickadee Cove and met him. But we weren't staying long, and I knew that if I met Aaron, I would one hundred percent neglect all of you."

"I'm just glad Lily is having good company for once in her life," Emily said. "The girl always chooses the worst people to hang out with."

"I'm surprised she even said yes to Reuben," Sarah added. "Knowing Lily, she always goes for the bad guys. And you say Reuben is a nice kid."

"She might not see it yet, but they match each other," Jeannie explained. "He knows what to say to keep Lily quiet, and I tell you, when they start exchanging words, there is no stopping them. They could be at it for hours. There's a spark between them. It's obvious."

"I hope so," Sarah voiced. "Maybe that way, Lily can finally stop getting into all sorts of trouble."

"Has she said anything about going back to New York, mum?" Emily inquired.

"No," Jeannie answered. "Which surprises me. I'm worried that soon, she'll start talking about returning, but I'm hoping that she'll find a reason to stay instead. You know if she were to return to her life in New York, she'd go back to her friends, the modeling, partying...I don't even want to think about it."

"Me, neither," Sarah said. "So, the plan is to make her fall so madly in love with this Reuben that she'll stay, right?"

Jeannie rolled her eyes. "No, Sarah."

"It won't work, 'cos eventually, Reuben will have to go back to school," Mason explained. "But look on the bright side. I mean, it's been two months, I think. She hasn't said anything about leaving. That should count for something."

"Yes, but she was recovering," Sarah said. "Now that she's all better, who knows what her plan is?"

"Should I talk to her about it?" Jeannie asked. "I mean, I fear that if I bring it up, she might think I'm trying to make her leave. I'm not so sure what to do."

"You know what? Don't think about his now, mum," Sarah told her. "Dress up, get pretty, and go on your date. You still recall all the pointers I gave you on how to do your makeup, right?"

"I do." Jeannie smiled. "Plus, Lily is here, so she can help me."

"Good. Have fun," Mason said. "We'll call you in the morning to ask how the double date went. And mum, don't let Lily mess things up with Reuben. Aaron says he's a nice guy, and I believe him. Hopefully, some of his goodness will rub off and Lily and she'll start acting her age."

Jeannie sighed. "Hopefully. Talk later. Bye, loves."

"Bye, mum," they chorused.

Just as she ended the call, Jeannie heard the doorbell ring. She sucked through her teeth and checked the time. Aaron and Reuben were an hour early.

Lily poked her head into the room through the crack in the door. "I asked Reuben to come an hour early so I could see what he decided to wear," she said. "Plus, I figured I'd talk to him for a bit to get to know him better."

Jeannie dropped her shoulders. "You really like Reuben, don't you?"

"Like is a strong word."

"It's really not." Jeannie shook her head.

"I know," Lily said, giggling. "But he's alright. He's a pretty boy, too, so he's my type. I feel like we have a lot in common, and we just need to talk about it. I personally don't know the things I like, so I'm thrilled to figure that out with him."

"I'm glad. Now, don't keep him waiting."

Jeannie heard Lily's footsteps running down the hall. She shook her head and turned back to the mirror. For her dress, Jeannie had gone for a nice, knee-length dark green gown with a Bardot neckline.

Soon, Jeannie had finished with her simple makeup and she was almost ready to go. She hadn't decided what to do with her hair, but she figured Lily would take care of it when she was done with hers.

*Speaking of Lily...*

Jeannie hadn't heard a thing in a while. For two people who bickered a lot, they were awfully quiet in the living room. Jeannie rose to her feet and made her way out of the room to figure out what was going on.

"Lily?" Jeannie said immediately as she walked into the room.

Strangely, Lily was asleep. On the couch. In an odd position. With Reuben nowhere in sight. Jeannie took slow steps forward, unsure of what was going on. The door was still open, and cold air was getting in. Confused, Jeannie went to shut it.

"Took you long enough."

Jeannie jumped, startled by the voice. She turned around and almost tripped on air when she saw Luka in her kitchen smirking.

"Hello, Jenny."

---

"What do you think you're doing here?"

Jeannie's throat had gone dry. Lily wasn't asleep. There was no way she could be. Luka had done something to her, something she didn't want to imagine. Still, she reckoned it was best to keep her cool. The last thing she wanted was to say something that would cause Luka to react badly.

"Come on, Jenny. You really don't know why I'm here?" he asked, strolling out of the kitchen. "Think."

"Don't call me that," Jeannie said softly. "What did you do to Lily?"

"What could I possibly do to Lily?" he asked, approaching her. "She's my daughter. I could never hurt her. Never. You managed to brainwash her and turn her against me, but that's not Lily's fault."

Jeannie took a step back. "What do you want from me, Luka? Why won't you please leave me alone? You can go. You have your whole life to live. Why won't you leave me alone! Leave me alone, Luka. Please."

"Ouch," Luka said, smirking. "I always tell you this, Jeannie. You always think only of yourself and what you want. We could have been happy if you had just accepted me back. We could have had a normal family. Like Lily wanted. But you got a restraining order against me? You treated me like a stalker. A nuisance. You tricked me."

Jeannie felt tears well up in her eyes. She was frustrated. Extremely tired and unable to think. "What did you do to Lily? Tell me what you did to her!"

"What I'm about to do to you."

Before Jeannie could grasp his statement, Luka reached for her and held her in a chokehold. Jeannie fought him, trying to pry away from his grasp, and she saw him reach into his pocket and pull out a white napkin. She stopped clawing at his hand over her neck with her fingers and attacked his wrist instead. Jeannie tried to push his hand away from her face so Luka couldn't cover her face with it. But the more she struggled, the tighter his hold on her neck became.

To her rescue, the door pushed open and Reuben

appeared. The smile he had on his face dropped faster than the bouquet of flowers in his hand.

"Jeannie," he stuttered as his breathing became labored.

"Run, Reuben," Jeannie managed to say. "Get help."

Swiftly, Luka threw Jeannie to the ground and charged for Reuben, who had frozen on the spot instead. Thankfully, Reuben quickly recovered from his shock. Before Luka could reach him, he managed to duck and grab Luka by the waist.

"Reuben," Jeannie said with a croaked voice, struggling to breathe. She wanted to tell him to be careful, but she couldn't speak.

Luka flung Reuben to the side of the room and he crashed into a small table. But he didn't stay down. Reuben staggered to his feet and charged for Luka again. Jeannie was torn between going to check on Lily or helping Reuben. She struggled to get on both feet and struggled even more to think of a course of action.

"Think, Jeannie. Think…"

Her phone.

Jeannie raced into her bedroom shaking. She had to call for help. She and Reuben were never going to defeat Luka on their own. She needed to call the police.

Quickly, Jeannie dialed 911 and sat on the floor, waiting to be connected.

"911, what is your emergency?"

"Yes, good evening. My name is Jeannie Miller. I and my daughter and her boyfriend are in trouble. A man. Luka Smith. My ex-husband. I have a restraining order against him but he's here. He knocked my daughter unconscious, and he is beating up Reuben, her boyfriend. I'm in the bedroom. Please send help. He really wants to hurt us."

"I need you to stay calm, miss. Are you hiding?"

"Yes…no, I'm in my room. I ran into the room to get my phone."

"Did you lock the door?"

Jeannie gasped and instantly rose to her feet. "No."

"Lock it."

Before she could even take a step forward, Luka stormed into the room holding the table lamp. He glared at her and dropped the lamp to the floor.

"He's here," she whispered into the phone, feeling a draft of cold air sweep into the room.

Luka grabbed her by the hair, pulled her to him, and covered her face with the chloroform-soaked napkin. She couldn't even struggle. The fear had crippled her, and the substance knocked her out in seconds.

$$Chapter\ Eighteen$$

There was a loud white noise ringing in Jeannie's ear. She found it difficult to lift her head. Her eyes were open, but she couldn't see a thing. Her throat was dry, and her nose was irritated. Jeannie groaned softly, struggling to stay awake. Soon enough, her eyes cleared, and she could finally get a good look at where she was.

"What..." she mumbled.

She was in a moving vehicle. A van. A spacious van. Luka was driving. Their hands were tied behind their backs with zip ties at the back of the van. The three of them. Her, Lily, and...

"Reuben," she whispered.

He was fully awake and staring at her. Reuben shook his head, trying to tell her not to say anything so Luka wouldn't notice they were awake. He lifted his head slightly and gestured to Luka with it, but Jeannie couldn't understand him.

"I see you're awake, Jeannie," Luka said, startling her. "The chloroform didn't keep you asleep for as long as I expected."

"Distract him," Reuben mouthed. "Untie me."

Jeannie nodded vigorously, reading his lips loud and clear. She adjusted and groaned as she struggled to sit up. "You, Luka...I honestly don't know what I did wrong in my life to deserve you."

She groaned, making it seem like she was in pain as she shifted to Reuben's side. Reuben had quietly turned around with his back to Jeannie, giving her access to his tied hands. Jeannie sat by him, close enough that she could touch the zip ties even though she couldn't see them.

"Who's that dude?"

Jeannie's heart skipped a beat. "What dude?" she asked.

"The boy next to you," Luka said. "The one who came to the house with flowers."

"Lily's boyfriend," Jeannie answered. "Why? Do you feel bad now that you knocked him unconscious with a lamp?"

Luka chuckled. "The boy can fight. I don't feel bad at all. I did what I could to win. He almost knocked me out with a punch, that sucker. I picked up the lamp because I got angry. I'll make sure to pay him back for that."

"No one in this van has ever wronged you, Luka," Jeannie said, clawing at the zip ties. She was hurting her fingers in the process, but she didn't mind. If it meant getting them out of the van, then Jeannie didn't mind bleeding.

"No one? You shouldn't be saying that to me, Jeannie Miller. *You* wronged me. You are the main culprit," Luka said, keeping his eyes on the road. "You took my children from me, you took my life. I understand that we had our differences. I understand why you are angry at me. But you had no right to turn my kids against me. Especially Lily. You had no right to do that."

"I did nothing. You did it all yourself, you lunatic," Jeannie said. "Who was it that slept with Mason's teacher and caused Mason to be the laughingstock of his class? Who was it that forgot to pick up his own daughter from school and let her get kidnapped? You don't get it, Luka! What you did, they saw it. They lived it. I didn't have to do anything. They watched Lily change from being a bubbly little girl to a depressed one and till this day, we don't know why it happened. We don't know what they did to her. She doesn't even remember, but she has to live with the consequences of your actions every single day. If you had not forgotten to pick her up from school that day, she wouldn't have changed. She wouldn't be battling depression, anorexia, and some other medical conditions that have cost me a fortune to treat. You ruined us, Luka."

"Shut it," Luka rasped. "You love to blame people, don't you, Jeannie? I admit I did some bad things, but how about you take the blame for the things you did."

Jeannie sighed, trying to mask her relief that she'd managed to loosen Reuben's zip tie. "I don't want to sound narcissistic, Luka. But I am flawless when it comes to our children. They are a blessing to me, and the only mistake I made was not cutting you out of their lives sooner. Take the blame? I have none. I tried and I succeeded in raising them the right way. My kids are successful now. They are living good lives, and I am so glad that you are unable to manipulate your way into their lives now. I'm so glad that they are stronger than me."

As she talked, trying to stall Luka, Reuben was busy untying the zip tie around his leg. Jeannie felt a lump in her throat watching him. She didn't know what their course of action was, but the first step was to break free, and Reuben was close to doing just that.

"Well, you better start practicing," Luka announced. "Because you will share some of the blame. I don't care what you have to do. You will get my children to love me again. You can tell them whatever. Tell them you chased me away, you abused me…I don't care. Just fix this or I swear, I will make your life a living hell."

Jeannie arched her eyebrows. "That's your plan? You sincerely think they will believe you? You're forgetting the part where they—"

Reuben shouted and charged for Luka in the blink of an eye. Jeannie hadn't realized that he had cut the ties loose. He grabbed Luka from behind, choking him. The car started to swerve. Left and right, in sharp turns. Luka struggled to keep the car on the road, breathe, and fight Reuben off. He succeeded to do none of those things. The car swerved off the road and hit a tree with so much force, Jeannie hit her head on the door and instantly, she lost consciousness.

---

The white noise again. It was louder this time. Jeannie couldn't hear anything else. The pain in her head had intensified, her entire body ached, and she felt something trickling down the side of her face.

"Lily? Reuben?" she managed to say.

She was still inside the van, but Lily and Reuben were gone. Jeannie's blood chilled at the thought of Luka kidnapping her daughter and Reuben. She staggered and struggled to get out of the empty van. Everything was spinning, and she could barely walk in a straight line, but Jeannie kept moving. She had to follow them. They couldn't have gone far.

How long had she been asleep?

A sigh of relief slipped from her lips when she saw Lily standing by the tree where the van had crashed into it. She was in Reuben's arms, sobbing. Reuben stroked her hair and patted her back, trying to console her. For a moment, Jeannie didn't want to interrupt them. It wasn't every day that she got to see her daughter vulnerable with someone.

"So, I don't deserve love? Even a little bit?" Jeannie asked, grabbing their attention. "You both are here consoling each other and you left me to sleep in the van. Alone. That's cold."

"Mum!" Lily screamed.

Her first instinct was to recoil, but Jeannie stood still instead. She waited and watched Lily run up to her. Lily wrapped her arms around Jeannie's waist and held on to her tightly.

"Did I die and go to heaven?" Jeannie joked.

"Are you alright?" Lily asked her, sobbing. "Your head is bleeding."

"Oh, I'm fine." Jeannie smiled. "I'm much better now after receiving a hug from you. "How are you?"

"A bit dizzy," Lily sniffed. "And my arm started to hurt again, but other than that, I'm fine."

"Reuben, how are you?" Jeannie asked him when she reached them.

"I'm alright, Jeannie," he answered. "Does your head hurt a lot?"

"No," she answered. "Tell me, Reuben. Are you really alright? I want to know where it hurts."

"Everywhere," he said. "But I'll live."

Jeannie nodded and scanned the area. "Where's Luka?"

"He took off," Lily answered. "When the car crashed, I regained consciousness for a few seconds and I saw him get out of the car."

"When I woke up, he was gone," Reuben answered. "I called the police. They should be here any minute now with an ambulance. I called Aaron, too. He's on his way."

"Mum, I'm so sorry this happened," Lily said as she started to cry again. "I should have been more careful about opening the door. I didn't know it was him. When I opened the door, he smiled, and I thought it was a friendly visit, but before I could say anything, he muffled me and I—"

"It's alright, my darling," Jeannie said. "I should have seen this coming."

"Now I understand why you got that restraining order," Lily said. "He's a nutjob. It scares me that my own father is a complete nutjob. What was he planning to do to us? What if we didn't escape? He barely knows Reuben. What would he have done to him, mum?"

Jeannie stroked Lily's hair. "We should thank Reuben," she said and turned to him. "Apparently, saving my life runs in the family. First it was Aaron, and now you. Thank you, Reuben. I honestly have no idea how we would have survived this without your help. You are a brave one."

Reuben smiled. "I did what I could. I'm just glad we're all safe. For a moment, I thought it was a bad decision to attack him when he was driving, but all I could think of was something my dad always told us. If you are ever held hostage, never let them take you to another location. If you must fight, then fight. But don't let them take you anywhere else. Because if they do, the chances of rescue become slim."

"You're right," Jeannie said. "Knowing Luka, he was probably driving us out of town. If he had succeeded, then it would have been days before they found us."

"What did he want, mum?" Lily asked, still holding on to Jeannie.

"You...your siblings," Jeannie sighed. "He says I ruined his life when it was the other way around. I don't know what happened to your father, Lily. He was not always like this. The Luka I met when I was a teenager was a nice boy. Money changed him. I don't how, but it drastically changed him. He became a totally different person, far from the Luka I knew."

"I feel like I caused this," Lily said. "I wanted our family back together, and I was being selfish about it. I think—"

"It's not you," Jeannie told her. "If anything, Luka used you, too. He thinks he owns me, and that's my fault. I'm ashamed of the many times I took him back, Lily. He got used to it. He'd leave, come back, beg, woo me again, and I accepted. He did it continually and it worked. Then, when he found out that I'd moved on, he got obsessed. He doesn't want our family back together, Lily. He wants to win. This is a game for him. One he has always won. Until now."

"Jeannie, if I may ask…" Reuben chimed in. "You can decide not to answer, but—"

"Ask whatever you want, Reuben," she told him.

"Why did you take him back so many times if he kept hurting you?" he asked. "I heard all you said in the van, and honestly…it was a lot. What he did to Lily, to you, to Mason. Mason is Lily's older brother, right?"

"Yes," Jeannie answered.

"So, if he cheated on you, then…how did you have Lily? You took him back after that, too, and got pregnant? After he humiliated and cheated on you? Why did you wait so long to cut ties with him?"

Jeannie swallowed, ashamed to even think of an answer. She had asked herself that question so many times in the past sixteen years. Why did she stay so long when it would have just been easier to cut ties with him?

"Because of us," Lily answered on her behalf. "Well, before I was born, it was because of Emily, Mason, and Sarah. You see, my mum here used to be a very optimistic person. At least, that's what Emily told me. She always had hope. She struggled and persevered for us. Mum went through a lot to train us. But you see, people used to bully my siblings for not having a father figure in the home. Mum took him back all those times because she thought he'd stay. Because she thought they needed him. But soon she realized that she could be both a mother and a father to us. That's when she decided to get a divorce. I didn't understand it before, but I do now. Sometimes letting go is the hardest thing to do."

"I'm sorry, Jeannie," Reuben said.

"There's nothing to be sorry for," Jeannie said, smiling as tears rolled down her cheeks. "I just pray to God that we get rid of Luka from our lives forever. He was gone for fifteen years once. I don't understand why he won't just disappear again."

"It's like you said. He's obsessed," Reuben explained. "But this time, he won't have it easy. He will be charged with assault, harassment, a restraining order violation, and kidnapping. He's looking at years in prison when he gets caught."

"I hope he gets caught soon," Lily said.

A car zoomed into the bushes and came to a sharp halt. Jeannie recognized one of Aaron's cars and a feeling of relief washed over her entire body. They were safe now. No one could harm them anymore.

"I'll kill him," Aaron said, stepping out of the car. "I promise you, I will kill him with my own hands. I apologize to you, Lily, but if I find your father, I will strangle him for this."

"You can get in line, Aaron. There's about…five people ahead of you," Lily said. "I'm pretty sure if Mason found out about this, he'd go in search of Luka himself."

"You're right. Mason is scary when he's angry," Jeannie said to Lily before turning her attention to Aaron. She sank into his arms and shut her eyes. "My head is bleeding."

"I see that," he said. "Do you feel dizzy?"

"No," Jeannie mumbled.

"Are you sure?" Aaron said, prying her off his body. "Look at me, Jeannie. How's your vision?"

"Clear," she answered, staring straight at him. "Reuben saved our lives."

Aaron smiled proudly. "Are you hurt, son?"

"A bit," he said. "But I'm alright."

"Are you sure?"

Reuben nodded. "If my dad hears that I saved two ladies, he's going to tell all the neighbors, and then they won't let me hear the end of it. I'm already popular as it is. I don't need all this fame."

Lily giggled and went in for a hug. "You should get used to it. You're a hero now. I'm pretty sure you'll be on the news. Your uncle is a big personality here, and his girlfriend was kidnapped."

"You're right," Reuben said, stroking her hair. "They might want to interview me."

"Do you need help writing your speech? I can help," Lily said to him.

"That's nice." Reuben smiled, staring down at Lily. "I'd like that."

Jeannie turned her attention from them to Aaron. "You got here faster than the ambulance and the police combined. Impressive."

Aaron wrapped his arms around her neck and sighed. "I'm just glad you're safe. When Reuben called me, I could barely think."

Jeannie moaned and shut her eyes. "This feels nice. I might just fall asleep."

"Whoa, that's not a good sign," Aaron said, holding her at arm's length. "Jeannie, keep your eyes open. You can't fall asleep."

"I can't help it," she mumbled.

She could hear Aaron talking, but his voice began to sound like an echo. It felt as if she were sinking into a deep, black hole, farther and farther away from the light. Soon, the light was as small as the moon from a distance, and then it became as small as a star...until eventually, everything became pitch black.

# Chapter Nineteen

*Two weeks later...*

"I don't think I've ever seen my uncle this happy."

"Oh, come on. He was married before he met my mum, I'm sure he was happy then."

"Did your mum not tell you the story of my uncle's last marriage?"

"What story?"

Reuben shook his head and clicked his tongue. "I'll tell you all about it later, but I can tell you this now. My dad always talks about it from time to time. He would often insult Uncle Aaron's dead wife, too. Call her names. He says she ruined uncle's life."

"Goodness," Lily said and turned to Reuben. "No wonder he matches so well with my mum. They have both been traumatized in their former marriages. It makes sense now."

"My dad even said that uncle's wife used to flirt with other men in front of Uncle Aaron," Reuben continued. "And the worst part was that Uncle Aaron really loved his wife. She was his first love."

"Aww," Lily cooed. "Getting your heart broken by your first love is a different kind of hurt."

"Tell me about it. Uncle Aaron was so shattered, he didn't date for years. I think he was so scarred that he became scared of commitment."

Jeannie leaned to her side. "Would you two stop gossiping about my boyfriend, please?"

Lily gasped sharply. "You can hear us? We were trying to whisper."

"Well, you both are bad at whispering," Jeannie said in a hushed tone. "Now, Aaron will be back any minute now with the wine, so shush. You should have just ended the conversation at the first sentence."

"Sorry," Reuben whispered.

For their double date, Aaron had taken them on his yacht to have dinner. Lily had been the first to jump on the idea. She had never been on a fancy yacht before. After the incident with Luka, they had spent days getting treated. Apparently their injures were more severe than they had imagined. Jeannie suffered a concussion and a fractured wrist, Lily suffered a concussion, too, and her arm had to be put back into the cast. Reuben had hurt his neck and his knee, and he had a wound at the back of his head from where Luka hit him.

The date was necessary. Jeannie was glad that Aaron decided to have it on his yacht. Truth be told, she was still paranoid.

Luka had still not been found.

It was a mystery how he'd managed to evade the police when there was a statewide search for him. Jeannie feared he might appear at any time, so she and Lily were living with Aaron in his home. Aaron had employed private protection for them at the shop, at the house, and a personal bodyguard for each of them. When he had announced it, Jeannie didn't even try to argue with him. It was necessary, and she was thankful for it. At least, if Luka tried to get to them again, he would have to go through someone his own size who was trained to fight.

"Sorry for the delay," Aaron apologized, holding an expensive bottle of wine. "But here it is."

"If I may ask, uncle," Reuben said. "Not to sound ungrateful, but...why do we need expensive wine? I mean, I get we are at a nice dinner. But that wine costs more than your car. And your car is expensive."

Aaron poured the wine into their cups, and he remained standing. "Because it's a special night."

"Why is it a special night?" Lily asked, leaning on the table.

"Yes, do tell. Why is it a special night, uncle?" Reuben asked, copying Lily's move by placing both hands on the table."

Jeannie snorted, amused. She decided to follow suit and leaned on the table, too. "Tell us, my love. Why is it a special night?"

Aaron stared at them and then shrugged his shoulders. "If you don't want the wine, then fine. I'll just take it back."

"No, no," they chorused.

"We have a right to be curious," Lily said. "You can just tell us so I can stop pretending like I didn't see a receipt from Blue Nile."

Aaron's jaw dropped. "You funny little girl."

"Blue Nile?" Jeannie asked, confused. "What is that?"

Reuben and Lily exchanged looks and began to shriek. It seemed as though everyone knew what Lily was talking about except Jeannie.

"No wonder you brought out the wine," Reuben said. "Oh, my dearest uncle."

"Alright, I'm starting to think it was a terrible decision to bring you here to Chickadee Cove to meet Lily. Both of us as a team have been a menace. But before you ruin the surprise..."

Aaron pushed his chair aside and got on one knee in front of Jeannie. He reached into his pocket and pulled out a small box. "Jeannie..."

"Oh my goodness," Lily gasped. "Reuben...Reuben it's happening. I guessed it, and I was right. You owe me ten bucks."

"Hush," Jeannie said to Lily and Reuben. Her heart was swelling with excitement as she rose to her feet.

"Jeannie," Aaron said again.

"Yes," Jeannie sang. "Yes, Aaron? I'm listening."

Aaron laughed and then inhaled deeply, trying to gather himself. "Alright. Let's do this. Jeannie Miller, you are the best thing that has happened to me in over a decade."

"Aww," Lily and Reuben cooed, holding onto each other's hands.

"From the very first day you walked into the sawmill confused, stressed, and agitated, I knew that you had captured my heart."

"Aww," they cooed again.

"I love you so much," Aaron continued. "You are strong..."

"I try to be," Jeannie whispered.

"You have a good heart, and you are selfless. When I'm around you, I'm always at peace. I want it to be this way forever. Will you please do me the honor and marry me, Jeannie? Let's do forever, together."

"Say yes, say yes," Lily and Reuben sang.

"Yes," Jeannie answered without hesitation. "Aaron, there is no doubt in my mind. I promise I'll be better for you. I will communicate better, I will tell you everything, I will support you, I will do my best to make you happy. You'll see."

Aaron slipped the ring onto her finger, rose to his feet, and hugged Jeannie. "Thank you," he whispered to her. "And thank you to my cheerleaders, Lily and Reuben. I cannot wait to send you both away to the Bahamas before you drive me insane."

Lily gasped. "You're sending the both of us?"

"Well, he's sending all of you," Jeannie explained. "You, Reuben, Emily, Sarah, and Mason. We're still making the arrangements. But the sooner you leave, the better. You almost ruined the surprise."

"No, we made it better," Reuben said. "We added the suspense, the intrigue, the soundtrack."

"Enough of that," Lily said. "Can we toast now?"

"Right," Aaron said and picked up his cup. "To this wonderful day, to my wonderful children, and to us, Jeannie. A toast. Cheers."

Jeannie raised her glass and then downed the contents. She was full of excitement, and it was difficult to contain it when all she wanted to do was leap for joy. With every single day that passed, Jeannie was convinced that she couldn't love Aaron any more than she already did. Yet, her love for him seemed to be increasing every day. None of her worries mattered anymore. The thought of a future as Mrs. Horn sent tingles down Jeannie's spine.

---

"Their plane should have landed, right?"

"Yes, my love."

"So, they'll be here any minute?"

"Yup."

Jeannie threw her head back and groaned. "You know, there was a time when I used to beg my children to visit me.

Now I fear Lily coming back because she's going to start taunting me again. That girl is an actual bully, Aaron."

Aaron chuckled. "I think she got worse when Reuben arrived. It's like we brought Annie and Haley from *The Parent Trap* together. I fear those two have become inseparable."

"It's your fault. You brought Reuben for this very reason."

"I brought Reuben here because I wanted Lily to make friends with my nice nephew. But she brought out the menace in him, and now they are a team."

Jeannie giggled and leaned on Aaron's shoulders. "I do miss them, though."

"Me, too," Aaron said. "This house has been so quiet the last two weeks. It's boring."

"Well, things are about to get interesting. The wedding is coming up, and we are going to have to sit down and plan it with our children," Jeannie said, sat up, and clasped Aaron's cheeks between her palms. "Now, I know you love me, Aaron. But you gotta promise me that you will still love me after you have a conversation with all my children at once."

Aaron snorted. "What are you saying, Jeannie?"

"Just promise me that you won't back out of the wedding," Jeannie asked.

"I'd never back out," Aaron answered. "Trust me, I can handle the kids. You've told me once before that they tend to bicker a lot."

"Yes, they do. They do, Aaron, and sometimes, it's too much," she said. "You might need to have an aspirin nearby. Just in case."

"Don't worry." Aaron chuckled. "I already love the kids, and they love me. We're good."

Just then, one of the bodyguards walked into the living room. "They have arrived, Aaron."

"Great," Aaron said, excited. "Please have their bags taken

to their respective rooms and ask the bodyguard we assigned to each of them to make themselves known."

"Right away," the bodyguard said and exited.

"Mother!"

"Oh dear," Jeannie said, chuckling.

"Dearest mother of mine," she heard Mason sing. "We are back from the Bahamas."

"We are back!" Lily shouted.

They walked into the living room one at a time. Lily was the first to run up to Jeannie and give her a big hug that caused Jeannie to lose her balance. Then Mason joined in, then Emily and Sarah.

"We missed you," Emily said. "But we had such a good time."

"You can't even imagine, mum," Lily said. "It was epic. Reuben kissed a dolphin."

"He did?" Jeannie giggled. "Did you take a picture?"

"Of course. I'll show you."

"Later," Mason said. "Now, I see someone responsible for the two weeks' vacation we just had and enjoyed. Mum, if you would please do the honor of introducing us to this fine gentleman."

Jeannie turned to Aaron and smiled. "Aaron, this is Mason, Emily, and Sarah. In person. Guys, this is Aaron Horn, my fiancé."

"You're a lot bigger in person," Sarah commented.

They went in for a hug at the same time, like they did to Jeannie. Aaron couldn't stop laughing. He hugged them back as his eyes filled with happy tears.

"It's a pleasure to meet you all in person," he said when they broke the hug. "Sorry it took so long."

"We should be the ones apologizing," Emily said. "We should have visited you the first time we came."

"It's totally fine. I'm glad we're meeting now."

"Isn't it odd that I was the last to know about him, yet I was the first to meet him?" Lily noted. "Plus, I'm his favorite. You can ask him, and he won't deny it."

"Keep dreaming," Mason said and turned back to Aaron. "We have a lot to catch up on, Aaron. We haven't spoken in two weeks."

"Your house is incredibly nice, Aaron," Sarah noted. "It's huge."

"Thank you," Aaron said. "Please make yourself at home. When you're ready, the bodyguards will show you to your rooms. Now, if you will please excuse us. Mason and I have something to do."

"You're going to talk about soccer, aren't you?" Jeannie asked.

"Yes, mum," Mason answered. "Yes, we are."

"Don't keep Aaron for too long," Lily said. "I need to tell him all about the trip."

Jeannie shook her head. "We need to talk about the wedding. We've started preparing, but there's still some things left to discuss. Like what you all will be wearing if you have guests coming..."

"Tomorrow," Emily said. "We're jetlagged, mum."

"Fine," Jeannie said. "Reuben, come on. Let's go to the kitchen. I'll make you some cookies and you can tell me all that happened on the trip."

"I would love to," Reuben said and rose to his feet. "Lily did some questionable things."

"Why, Reuben?" Lily asked.

"Because he won't lie to me, and I like his company."

"Well, I'm coming with," Lily said. "Reuben and I are inseparable now."

"Sarah and I are going to find our rooms," Emily said. "This is the first time in my life that I've had a bodyguard.

And it's all thanks to my father, who might just decide to wake up one morning and kidnap one of us."

"I still don't understand why the police haven't found him yet," Sarah said.

"We will talk about that later," Jeannie said, taking Reuben by the arm. "For now, get some rest, eat, and freshen up. We have a lot to do before my wedding. A lot."

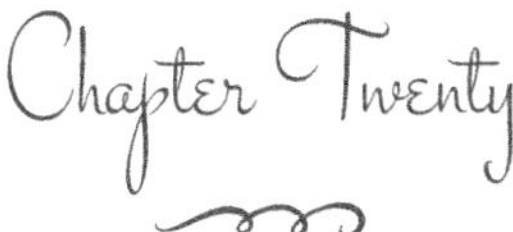

# Chapter Twenty

"I'm serious. Take it from someone who travels a lot," Sarah said. "Bali isn't the best place for their honeymoon. I think they should go to the Maldives."

Jeannie had taken a dose of aspirin before coming down for the meeting, but she feared Aaron didn't take her advice. They had been seated at the dining table for over an hour and had barely gone past the first topic of discussion on the list.

Aaron massaged his temple. "Guys—"

"The Maldives isn't even a destination anymore. Anyone can go there. It's not romantic," Lily argued.

"Yes, it is," Sarah said. "It has luxurious resorts, white sand beaches, and clear blue waters. It's like waking up in paradise."

"It's a beach. Nothing more," Lily said.

"Like you've been there before."

"I've seen pictures."

"I've been there in the flesh."

"Big whoop."

"Okay, Lily," Reuben called her and took her wrist. "I need you to sit back down and relax."

Lily took in a deep breath and obliged. Jeannie smiled at

Reuben, impressed that he could get Lily to stop yelling. Usually, when she started like that, it always ended in her storming out of the room.

"Okay, so I'm against the Maldives, too," Emily said.

"Ha!" Lily yelled.

"But...let me finish," Emily continued. "It's a good suggestion, so we will write it down. For me, I think they should go to Bora Bora. It's paradise."

They were trying to decide where Jeannie and Aaron were going to have their honeymoon. One would think that the couple would have the liberty of deciding where they wanted to go, or if they wanted to go at all, but not in Jeannie's case. Her children decided. They took it upon themselves mainly because they'd decided to sponsor the honeymoon.

"What is with you girls and beaches?" Mason asked. "Look, mum isn't a girl, and Aaron is a mature man. You can't expect them to enjoy things like you do."

"Which is exactly why I think we should decide ourselves," Jeannie chimed in. "This can wait. We have other—"

"Stay out of this, mum," Sarah asked. "Bora Bora is a good idea, too. I haven't been there yet, but it is on my bucket list."

"What about Paris?" Reuben spoke up. "It's simple, iconic."

"Paris is stressful, Reuben," Mason said. "We need somewhere they can relax. I don't think they want to spend their honeymoon sight-seeing."

Aaron finally cleared his throat. "Well, actually—"

"Aaron, you have to stay out of this, too," Mason told him. "We know these things because we travel a lot. Let's decide what's best for you both, alright? It's the least we can do."

Aaron gave Jeannie a baffled look that caused her to laugh. She had warned him, but he refused to listen.

"Let's think, guys," Emily said. "We need somewhere they

would love. Somewhere nice. This is our one shot at doing something nice for Aaron and mum. We cannot fail."

"What about China?" Lily suggested.

"Shut up, Lily," Sarah said.

"Don't tell me to shut up. It's a good suggestion."

"The language barrier would make it stressful for them," Emily explained. "Remember, we're looking for a place they can unwind."

"Why don't you ask us then?" Aaron tried a second attempt to chime in. "I mean, we will be the ones going on the honeymoon, so isn't it ideal that we pick the place?"

"No, uncle. Let us think," Reuben replied.

"I would have thought that you would take my and Jeannie's side, Reuben," Aaron said.

"We want what's best for you," he mumbled, then snapped his fingers. "Barbados."

They all gasped one by one, nodding. "I like that idea," Lily said. "Good job, Reuben."

"I'm thinking Cairo," Sarah said.

"Hawaii," Emily said.

"Ibiza," Mason added.

"The Grand Canyon," Reuben suggested.

"At this rate, we are never going to decide," Emily said. "We're not on the same page."

"How about Santorini, Greece?" Aaron said. "It's a group of islands. Your mum loves islands, and it's beautiful there, with one of the best sunsets."

"Why didn't I think of Santorini?" Sarah said, rising to her feet. "It's perfect. It's the most romantic."

Mason nodded and banged his hand on the table. "I like Santorini. It's beautiful."

"Then it is settled," Emily said. "We are sponsoring mum and Aaron's honeymoon to Santorini as their wedding gift.

Sarah, make all the necessary preparations. The wedding is less than a month away.”

“I’ll get right on it,” Sarah said. “After the meeting.”

“Now we move on to the next topic on our list,” Emily said, scanning the paper Jeannie had given her earlier. “Mum’s maid of honor.”

“What?” Jeannie blurted. “That’s not on my list. The next topic of discussion is food and drinks. We need to discuss a menu.”

“No, your maid of honor is the next topic to discuss,” Emily protested. “Now, I don’t think we will waste any time on this. I am mum’s first daughter, hence, it is my responsibility—”

“No, it’s not,” Lily said. “Why should you get to be the maid of honor? I want to be the maid of honor. If you think about it, I should be the first pick. When you left home in New York, I stayed with mum till she decided to move here and start the bakery. I’m the closest to mum.”

“That’s what you think,” Emily said. “But does it make any sense?”

“You guys,” Jeannie groaned. “Cathy will be my maid of honor.”

“No, she is not,” Sarah said. “No disrespect to Aunt Cathy, but she’s married, mum. Technically, she’d be a matron of honor, and it doesn’t sound right. You need a maid of honor. So you need to choose between Emily and Lily.”

“No. I will have a matron of honor then,” Jeannie said. “I’m not choosing. It’s Cathy. That’s final. Emily, Sarah, and Lily will be my bridesmaids. You all need to decide on a color later. Not here. Now, can we please discuss the menu? Reuben, honey, do you have any food allergies I need to know about?”

“No, Jeannie,” Reuben answered.

"Good," Jeannie said, sitting up. "So, Denise is going to be—"

"Why did you only ask Reuben?" Lily asked.

"Because I gave birth to all of you and I know your allergies," Jeannie said. "Now, as I was saying, Denise is going to be our caterer. She used to—"

"Wait a minute," Emily said. "What about the best man? Aaron has to choose between Reuben and Mason."

Aaron scanned the room awkwardly. He turned to look at Jeannie, hoping she'd say something, but Jeannie looked away. She knew Mason wanted to be the best man, but it had to be Reuben. It would be unfair not to pick him.

"I'll just pick someone at the office," Aaron announced.

"It's fine," Mason said. "I've only known you a few months, Aaron. Reuben is your best man. You've known him since he was born. It's not that deep."

Aaron inhaled sharply. "Actually, Reuben's dad is going to be in attendance, and he asked to be the best man, too."

"What?" Reuben said. "You're going to pick my dad over me?"

"It's his brother, what did you expect?" Lily asked. "Come on. I'll be a bridesmaid, you'll be a groomsman. It's perfect."

Jeannie's butt had gotten sore from sitting for too long. She knew this would happen. The scary part was that they hadn't even gotten to the topic she dreaded. Picking a color.

"Guys. Since that has been sorted, let's talk about something else. Like your outfits. You all need to decide on a color to match. Now, please, let's be considerate. I would have chosen a color and asked that you all cooperate, but I know you will not. So, what color are we going for? A neutral color?"

There was silence at first, and Jeannie wanted to believe that they were thinking about it. But deep down, she knew this was the calm before the storm.

"Emerald green," Sarah suggested.

"Green doesn't really go with my eyes," Reuben said. "How about blue? Ocean blue."

"No, too basic," Emily said. "Nude?"

"Brown," Lily said.

"I'm thinking black," Mason chimed in.

Sarah scoffed. "Is it a wedding or a funeral?"

Jeannie gave Aaron a knowing look and they both rose to their feet simultaneously. The argument intensified as Jeannie and Aaron strolled out of the room holding hands.

"They seem to be enjoying this," Aaron said. "How about we let them plan the wedding while we kick back and relax? They are enthusiastic about this."

"I agree," Jeannie said. "I'm sure they will decide eventually."

"In the end, we will still get married, right?"

"Right. But keep in mind, there is a slight possibility that we might have to elope," Jeannie teased.

Aaron chuckled. "I hope not. But jokes apart, I really... really love your children. This house is alive thanks to them."

"Really? You like all that noise?"

"Isn't it entertaining?"

"Well...it can be," Jeannie said. "But brace yourself. We're doing this forever, so you will have to get used to this, especially during Thanksgiving and Christmas."

Aaron placed a peck on Jeannie's cheek. "I look forward to it."

Jeannie Horn sighed in absolute relief. Earlier that day, the wedding bells had caused butterflies to invade her stomach. The happiest day of her life was also the day she almost peed her pants. Nothing had made her that nervous before. But when she said yes to Aaron, and the priest proclaimed them as man and wife, all the tension dissipated.

The reception had been so energy-consuming, Jeannie couldn't feel her legs. They had danced to different tunes, played games that Mason had organized, and laughed so hard at Emily's, Reuben's, Lily's, Mason's, and Sarah's speeches.

It truly was the happiest day of Jeannie's life.

"I packed some nice nightwear for you, mum," Sarah said and winked as soon as Jeannie rolled down the car window. "Have fun in Greece, mum. Please. Have some fun."

"Don't," Jeannie cautioned, sensing that Sarah was about to cry. "If you cry, I'll cry, and I look so beautiful today. I don't want to cry."

"I won't cry. Just hear me out," Sarah said. "I know the speech I gave inside the hall was funny, but there's something I need to add. You are an amazing mother, mum. You did your best. I know raising all of us broke you, but you managed to keep it together for us. I love you so much, and I will never forget the sacrifices you made to make sure we were educated."

There was no use holding back the tears. "I love you, too, Sarah," Jeannie sobbed. "Thank you."

Sarah kissed Jeannie on the cheek and scurried over to the other side of the car to say goodbye to Aaron, too.

"Hi, mum," Emily appeared. "You look nice."

"You've told me that about a hundred times today, Emily. But thank you."

"You're welcome," she said, almost in a whisper. "I'll make this quick. Have fun in Greece. I want pictures, alright?"

"Alright." Jeannie nodded.

"I'd like to say that I'm sorry," Emily continued. "I'm sorry for the life you lived, mum."

"Why are you all trying to make me cry?" Jeannie asked.

"Just hear me out," Emily asked. "This is a heartfelt goodbye. I might not see you again for another couple of months. As I was saying, I'm sorry you married Luka and had to suffer. But all that is over now. Although Luka is still somewhere out there, I'd' like to believe we have heard the last of him. Live your life, mum. You made a great choice with Aaron, and I wish you nothing but happiness. I pray that one day, I will find someone that loves me like Aaron loves you."

"I pray that prayer for all of you every single day," Jeannie said. "I love you, honey."

"I love you, too."

"My turn," Lily said and squatted by the car. "Hello, mother of mine."

"Hello, daughter of mine." Jeannie giggled. "I suppose you have something heartfelt to say."

"I have two announcements to make instead that I think will make you very happy," Lily said. "I have decided to stay in Chickadee Cove. I will go to New York sometime next week with Reuben to pack my things. I will work at the bakery while I take online classes for college. You're right. Reuben and I talked, and I decided that having a degree will be best, even if modelling is what I want to do. So I'll return to college."

Jeannie covered her face and cried. It took her a moment, but she was able to wipe her tears and gather herself. "I'm glad to hear that. When I get back, we'll talk more about your plans for your future, Lily."

"Okay," Lily whispered. "I love you, mum. Thank you for being patient."

"Thank you, Lily," Jeannie said.

"And I would like to add that moving to Chickadee Cove was the best decision you ever made, in case you hadn't noticed. Hopefully, Chickadee Cove will be good to me, like it was to you."

"I'll make sure of it," Jeannie said.

As the car drove down the road, Jeannie glanced at her five

children standing outside the hall, waving at them. It felt like she had hit a reset button in life. Now, she had everything she wanted. All in one man, and one town.

"Are you alright?" Aaron asked, pulling Jeannie into his embrace.

Jeannie hugged him tightly and shut her eyes.

"I'm happier than I've ever been, Aaron," she stated. "And I love you deeply."

"I love you, too, Jeannie Horn."

# About the Author

Eliza's a BIG believer in love. She writes sweet romances that make you swoon, laugh and believe in love again.

A mother of two children, Eliza and her husband of twenty-five years live in NH. She enjoys spending time with them and taking care of her many pets. When she isn't working on her next book, you can find her at the local nursery looking for the next hybrid tea rose to add to her garden.